Throwaway angels

NANCY RICHLER

PRESS GANG PUBLISHERS

VANCOUVER

The Publisher acknowledges financial assistance from the Canada Council, the Book
Publishing Industry Development Program of the Department of Canadian Heritage, and
the Cultural Services Branch, Province of British Columbia.

Canadian Cataloguing in Publication Data

Richler, Nancy, 1957–
Throwaway angels

ISBN 0-88974-062-3

   I. Title.
PS8585.I368T57   1996   C813'.54   C96-910551-7
PR9199.3.R5125T57   1996

Edited by Barbara Kuhne and Nancy Pollak
Copy edited by Robin Van Heck
Cover and text designed by Val Speidel
Author photograph by Vicki Trerise
Typeset in Monotype Bell
Printed by Best Book Manufacturers
Printed on acid-free paper
Printed and bound in Canada

Press Gang Publishers
#101 - 225 East 17th Avenue
Vancouver, B.C. V5V 1A6 Canada
Tel: 604 876-7787 Fax: 604 876-7892

For Rhea Lynne Schneiders

Acknowledgements

Thanks to:

Camilla Jenkins, Janet Richler Ostro, Diane Comet Richler,
Martin Richler, Dianne Richler, Shira Rosan, Jay Schneiders
and Aletha Worrall, who read the first draft of this novel and
offered encouragement and suggestions.

Angela Hryniuk, Lydia Kwa and Carmen Rodriguez
for their camaraderie and criticism.

The women at Press Gang Publishers for making this such
a positive and relatively painless experience.
Special thanks to Barbara Kuhne and Nancy Pollak
for their sharp yet tactful editorial input.

Myer and Dianne Richler
for their constant support and generosity.

Vicki Trerise—Anything I might say couldn't come close.

I am not a bold person, never have been. When it comes down to action—the grand gesture, the decisive deed—I admire it greatly, but would rather eat pie. And I do, every morning before work, at George's place on Hastings. Which is where I first heard what was happening.

"How's that redhead friend of yours?" George asked as I spread ice cream over my pie. I don't like big, melting lumps that go flying off the plate when you try to shave a bit off the side. I always squash it down, neat, and spread it around the top.

"What redhead?" I asked.

"I don't know her name. She had coffee with you a few times. Tall, kind of good-looking . . ."

"You mean Gem."

She wasn't really a friend. She was a customer, friendlier than most.

"I haven't seen her around," I said and realized it was true. She seemed to have dropped out as suddenly as she'd dropped in. "You should have said something sooner. I would have introduced you."

George didn't make the face he's supposed to when I tease him about women.

"Great pie, George," I said, just to loosen him up. Truth is, it was a little too sweet. "Where'd you find blackberries this time of year?"

George's face twitched, and he warmed up my coffee. He loves it when I comment on his baking. In that way, he's easy.

I ate my pie and started on the crossword while George waited on customers. Mornings are always busy at his place, especially rainy mornings, and being November in Vancouver, it was raining. The windows were fogged, and the air was heavy and close. All the stools at the counter were taken and almost all the booths. George was cool, though, whirling around doing five things at once. If you didn't know him well, you wouldn't even realize he was whirling.

Two cops came in while he was pouring fresh water into the coffee machine. He nodded and raised the pot in greeting while the two teenaged girls on the stools beside me scrambled to get moving. One turned her pockets inside out looking for money; her friend started rubbing her hands over her bald scalp—to wipe the sweat off her palms, or, maybe, just to make sure no hairs had managed to poke through while she was sitting there drinking her coffee. The one with hair found a handful of change and heaped it on the counter. Neither of them looked back as they beat it to the door. If they had, they would have seen one of the cops watching them and shaking his head. They'd be picked up and back with their parents within the day. Two days, tops. Which would either be a good thing, or not.

"So really," George said as he came around with more coffee, "do you know where she is?"

"Who?" I asked, then remembered. I covered the top of my cup with my hand. "I don't keep tabs on all my customers."

George shrugged. "I'm not the only one who wants to know."

I waited for him to get on with it. He waited for me to ask.

"Who wants to know?" I asked.

"Cops are looking for her," he said, shrugging again, as if it was no big deal to have the cops stopping by asking him questions.

"What do you mean, cops are looking for her? What for?"

My interest encouraged George. He shrugged even more nonchalantly than before. "Ask them," he said, jerking his head in their direction.

"C'mon," I begged.

George wiped the counter where the teenagers had been sitting.

"You're bullshitting," I said. "You just want me to get you together with her."

"You crazy?" he asked, and he looked me in the eye. I realized I'd hardly ever seen his eyes front-to-front like that. They were nice. Soft. "She bumped off a john."

"She's a social worker, George."

"I know what she is. And she's been tossing men into dumpsters. One anyway."

I nodded and tried to get my face still so I could think a bit in private. George studied my face, then, finding nothing, left me alone.

I knew about the man in the dumpster. Everyone did. SEX SLAYING, all the newspapers were screaming, as if this was a new concept for Vancouver. As if we hadn't already lost eight girls in the last two years alone. But this was a lawyer. West Side. Family man. It wasn't supposed to happen to him.

I hadn't been too upset over him. I'd actually even cheered a little. In private. Way to go, I secretly thought, one less asshole in the world. Of course, I had no proof he was an asshole. Just a strong hunch. The corn cob added a special touch, I thought. Personal.

I paid for my pie and remembered to leave a tip. I called good-bye to George and nodded at the two cops as I left. Probably they'd be by the laundromat over the next day or two to ask a few questions. Just routine.

The rain had eased to drizzle when I stepped outside. To the west, it looked like the sky might be clearing. The weatherman had promised a break before the next front moved in, but by the time I'd walked the six blocks to work, the drizzle was thickening to rain again. I pulled my jacket collar around my neck and kept my head down.

Josie was waiting at the door when I got to work. She always opens the place up with me, then spends the rest of the morning warming her hands on the radiator and telling anyone who will listen what she's seen the night before. Her cheeks and nose looked redder than usual, splotchier, like her skin was one layer closer to breaking down completely. Her kerchief was damp with rain or grease and had slipped too far down her forehead. I wondered how long she'd been waiting.

"Hi Jose," I said. She's very particular about who calls her Jose. Try it too soon and she'll spit in your face. I saw a customer get it once, right in the eye. Served him right, I thought. Not all lines are there to be crossed.

"Like my new umbrella?" Josie asked, waving it at me. It was the same one she always carried around with her. Maybe something had happened to it since yesterday, though.

"Yeah. Nice colour," I said as I unlocked the door. "That the one your brother gave you?"

"My brother gave it to me. He's a postie, you know." There are certain bits of information we go over every morning.

"Looks like the weather's not going to clear after all," I said.

Her head bobbed a bit, but she had already lost interest in the conversation. She took up her position by the radiator as I checked

4

the change machines, pulled lint out of the dryers and made sure no one had left laundry in any of the machines overnight.

Three customers came in right away. No one I knew or recognized. They already had soap and change so I sat behind the counter and worked on the crossword.

"My cat was poisoned," Josie said.

No one answered.

"Yup, right after Thanksgiving. Ginger, he was, but that didn't matter. They poisoned him anyway."

"Mmm," one of the customers responded as he started reading the newspaper.

The crossword wasn't going well. Some days they don't.

"Hi Josie," a familiar voice said. Gina, with a load that looked like she hadn't seen the inside of a laundromat for over a month. She had dyed her hair back to its original black since yesterday, and her face was all bone and blue eyes, like someone had drained her blood overnight.

"Hi hon," she said, leaning over the counter to brush her lips across my cheek. Rough as a cat's tongue, I liked how they felt. No one had touched me yet that morning.

"What's the matter?" she asked, jerking back. I wondered what she smelled.

"Nothing. What's the matter with you?"

She didn't answer.

I went over to her side of the counter to help her sort her clothes. She had just taken a job at Polly's Pets and everything about her smelled like cedar and wet wool. An improvement, I thought, over what she used to bring back from the bar, but she didn't agree. She hated everything about retail.

"How are you?" I asked. She was looking a bit hollow around the eyes, but it could have been the light.

She looked up from her laundry and wrinkled her nose.

"I'm thinking of filing a complaint against Xandu's," she said. Xandu's was the bar where she'd worked before Polly's. Not the worst of its kind. "I don't think they can fire me just for getting fat. I'm pretty sure it's discrimination or something. Don't you think?"

She winked, but I wasn't entirely sure she was kidding.

"Maybe because you were dancing, they can get away with rules about how you look," I ventured.

"Bullshit. There's no reason. None. If anything, I gave them *more* tits and ass for their money."

She had a point.

"Why don't you try speaking to Roger again?" I asked her. Roger was the manager.

"Because he's an asshole," she answered.

We both thought about that for a while as we separated out her brights. I don't know why we bothered. Her whites were all rat-grey anyway from all the times she hadn't bothered to separate.

"Cops came by this morning," Josie said from her radiator.

"I just want my job back," Gina continued, ignoring her.

"They came by here?" I asked.

Josie nodded.

"Fucking fleas," Gina said. "They're everywhere. They're even hanging around the bar now, asking questions. Lois told me."

"This morning they came by? Before I got here?" I asked.

Josie didn't respond. She looked straight at me, chewing at a bit of her upper lip.

"Don't worry," Gina said. "They'll be back."

I helped Gina cram her clothes into three washers. They were all too full. I was sure they'd unbalance mid-cycle, but she swore they'd be fine.

"You seen that tall redheaded woman who used to come in here last summer?" I asked Gina, as casually as I could, while she fitted her quarters into the slot. "Sort of friendly—I think she said she was some kind of a social worker."

Gina looked at me for a second. "Don't believe everything George tells you."

"So you don't buy it," I managed to say, surprised to find myself as disappointed as I was relieved.

"Do you?"

I thought about it. "I don't know. She *was* a bit strange. A bit *too* friendly."

"Oh for crissake. It doesn't mean she's a psycho. Maybe she liked you."

"Maybe." I didn't know what being a psycho had to do with anything. And I didn't know why I'd said she was too friendly. She was friendly. Period. Some customers are. She smiled when I gave her change, thanked me for soap, asked me out for coffee. Nothing strange in any of that. I'd figured she liked me.

"Fuck," Gina said, suddenly.

"Filthy girl," Josie muttered.

"Look," Gina said to me. "I have to be at the bloody zoo in fifteen minutes. I forgot I'm opening. Would you be a sweetheart and finish the load for me?"

I didn't mind. I always take some pride in transforming a dirty heap of clothes into a neat, sweet-smelling stack. I get very particular about lining up the edges, flattening out the creases, folding them just so. A customer once called it compulsive. I was helping Gem fold and this woman was watching. I thought she was admiring my technique, the quickness of my hands.

"You obviously have an anal-retentive need for order," she said after a while. Those were her exact words. She was a social worker, like Gem, but different from Gem.

I wish I'd told her to leave my ass out of it and stick it up her own, but I didn't think of that until later.

"What do you mean by a need for order?" I had asked instead.

"Look at the way you're folding those clothes," she said. "I mean, it's just like any other mindless, repetitive job—it keeps you busy and makes you believe you have control over something, which, of course, you don't. And the way you're concentrating. As if what you're doing actually matters."

"It does matter," Gem said, which I appreciated, especially since it was her clothes I was folding.

"Yeah, well," the bitch continued, "haven't you ever noticed that all the nice folded clothes come back each week with the same blood and shit all over them?"

"Sweat," I said. "They come back with sweat on them. Maybe a little blood, if someone's gotten her period, but mostly it's just sweat and grime."

She shook her head as if I'd missed the point. As if I was too stupid to have gotten it. But she was the one who missed the point. Which had to do with keeping things going, and preferring to fold clothes than to sell them, sew them or peel them.

"There's a special on tomatoes at Safeway," Josie broke into my thoughts. "Some of them are mouldy, but they're still good for sauce."

"Of course they're mouldy," I said, irritated at Josie, or Safeway, I wasn't sure which. I wished she would take her kerchief and coat off, instead of sitting all bundled and huddled as if she were on a park bench, or something. "Who ever heard of decent tomatoes in November?"

"I'm going to Safeway right after here," Josie said, as if I hadn't even spoken. "They're having a special on tomatoes all this week."

"I'm sure they're good for sauce," I said.

"Yes. Some of them are mouldy, but they're still good for sauce."

I'd noticed before that conversations always go Josie's way, and wondered, not for the first time, what would happen if they didn't.

The morning sped up with the ten o'clock rush. All the machines were in use, with customers waiting in line for more to come free. Everyone seemed to have forgotten to bring soap. From behind the counter, I could see a couple of customers overloading the machines, but with the lineup of people needing change, there was nothing I could do except yell out a warning. I knew one or more of the washers would break down from the stress of it all and, at 11:00, number five went. I got to work on it, but numbers eight and eleven went out before I'd even figured out if I could fix five. Most of the customers were patient, but a few sighed louder than they had to, as if it was my fault they had to choose the busiest time of the day to wash their clothes.

As I went to call for repair, I saw Josie rummaging through her purse.

"You can't smoke in here, Jose," I reminded her.

"You got a light?" she asked me.

"I don't have a light, and you know you can't smoke in here."

She looked at me for a moment, then clutched her coat closer around her and made for the door. It was a routine we repeated every day. I was tired of it.

At the first lull, I mopped the floor and opened the door to try to dry the place out a bit. It was still raining. I liked the sound of it hitting the pavement as I mopped near the door. Like fat in a frying pan, only clean. I wondered if Gem was listening to the same rain, or if she'd gotten far enough away to be dry.

Once, when she first started coming around, she showed me a picture of a girl. A young girl, thirteen or so, with a puffy face and flat eyes.

"Ever see her?" she asked me.

I shook my head. "She a relative of yours?" I asked. I could see a faint resemblance, a tightness around the corners of the mouth.

"Uh uh," Gem said. "Just a kid I'm looking for." She looked at the picture, then stared away. Her flat gold eyes were impossible to read. "She's been missing for a week."

"A runaway?"

Gem nodded.

"Maybe she's gone home."

"I doubt it."

"Where's she from?" I looked at the picture again, trying to imagine a kid with that face riding a bicycle or opening presents on Christmas. It was hard.

"Kamloops."

"Nothing wrong with Kamloops," I said. I think I was trying to be reassuring.

"Kamloops isn't the issue," Gem said through that tight mouth of hers.

"I know," I said, and we both shrugged at exactly the same time. There was nothing wrong with Kamloops. I'd been there a few times. The air was dry and sweet and the river was so clear you'd never know about the pulp mill. I hoped Gem was there now.

Josie was in a foul mood when she returned that afternoon. She didn't say anything, but her face was blurry and she didn't look my way as she took up her post by the radiator. With anyone else, I might have broken the ice by saying "Rough day?" or something like that, but Josie didn't like other people breaking her ice. I brewed a pot of coffee and put a mug of it on her radiator. I hadn't even turned around before she grabbed it with both her hands and brought it up to her face to inhale the steam.

The afternoon dragged. All the machines except one were fixed, but some were idle. I picked up the crossword and put it down again in irritation. I didn't see how anyone could be expected to know the answer to "Air: comb. form." Gina called at 3:00 to say she wouldn't be able to make it in to pick up her laundry. By 3:30 the grey pushing against the window was darkening. I had an irresistible urge to get a lungful of fresh air before dark, so I stood by the open doorway until Gina called back at 3:45 to say she would be in. It sounded like she was having the same kind of afternoon I was.

"How are things at Polly's?" I asked.

"Just hopping. Two puppies with kennel cough and a rush on goldfish."

After we hung up, I wondered why a rush on goldfish, out of nowhere, and called her back to ask.

"It's not out of nowhere. Some science teacher at Strathcona assigned a project on them. Fucking irresponsible if you ask me."

At 4:30, Gina called back to say she wouldn't make it in after all. "Polly's got her knickers all in a twist wondering why her fucking parrot keeps saying 'Fuck' all of a sudden."

"You have to stay late to talk about her parrot's vocabulary?"

"Yeah. And she thinks fifty dollars is missing from the till."

"Oh Christ. What's her problem?"

"I don't know, but it's about to become mine."

"Don't let her push you around," I said.

"Yeah, right."

When I got off the phone, Josie was rearranging her kerchief and muttering something about filthy girls.

"There are no filthy girls in here, Jose," I said and started counting the day's totals. By the time Marlene came in to relieve me, I was ready to go.

"Have you heard the latest?" Marlene asked me. She looked exhausted. Pertly dressed as usual, but a tinge of grey seeped through the mask of pink makeup she had spread across her face.

"Uh uh," I said, bracing for the latest bulletin about her estranged husband.

"Haven't you heard? They think they know who killed that guy in the dumpster."

I tensed, waited.

"Apparently the murderer—murderess, actually—was one of our customers. I don't remember ever seeing her, though. It's kind of creepy to think she might have been in here."

"What's creepy about it?" I turned half away from her so she couldn't see my hands shaking as I did up my coat.

"What's *creepy* about it?"

I understood for the first time why Josie always leaves at the end of my shift. I couldn't put my finger on why, but all of a sudden I just wanted to be outside, far away from Marlene and the sound of her voice.

"Nothing's creepy, I guess, if sick murderers don't bother you. And this one was *really* sick. Did you hear she impaled him?"

Of course I had.

"I mean, what kind of twisted bitch would mutilate someone like that?"

Josie was sidling toward the door.

" 'Night, Jose," I called.

"With a corn cob, for Christ's sake. I wonder if that was before or after she slit his throat."

" 'Night, Marlene," I said, and made for the door.

The rain had lightened to fine drizzle when I got outside, nothing serious enough to soak through my jean jacket. I walked slowly, trying to think, but couldn't. The evening felt nice falling wet against my face.

I followed Hastings east staying close to the curb. The road was busy with cars and buses speeding along the wet pavement, but the sidewalk seemed quiet for so early in the evening. Unusually quiet. The odd figure slouched by a storefront or huddled in a doorway. A woman here and there clung to her curb. I nodded to one I knew from the laundromat. She was dressed for work—high spiked heels, short tight skirt, bare legs, open throat, even in the rain. She didn't nod back. Gem's angels, I caught myself thinking. That's what she called us. The ones who make the coffee, wash the clothes, suck the cocks—the real work. I knew she was full of shit, condescending, even, but still, it made me feel good. No one had ever called me an angel before.

I turned up Gina's street and walked by her house. Hers was one of the last wood-frames still standing on that street. Wedged between a scrap-metal shop and a garage, it looked out of place. It couldn't last much longer, was already up for sale. *For knockdown*, Gina said, though at the moment it was only the "For Sale" sign out front that was knocked down. By Gina, I suspected.

Her light was on. I thought about stopping in but realized I wasn't in the mood. I wasn't in the mood to be alone either. I'd noticed, lately, that I often wasn't in the mood for any of the available options.

I turned onto my own street and saw they still hadn't replaced the streetlight that was out. I resisted the impulse to quicken my pace, kept walking slowly, my shoulders straight. I knew the street wasn't any less safe than it had ever been. It just felt that way.

When I got inside my building, I took a deep breath. The hallway smelled like a new tom had moved in. I let myself into my apartment and remembered to close the door quietly. 2-C had been complaining about me to the super. She said I was slamming the door. Purposely. Just to get to her. "It's not me that's getting to her," I told him, but something was. I closed the door very quietly, went through the mail, considered supper, and ran a bath instead.

As I lay in my bath the rain started again in earnest. One thing I do like a lot about my life is my bathroom. From the tub, which is old-fashioned and huge, I can lie back and look out the window. In the summer I watch clouds move across the sky and in the winter I watch the dark. If I keep the window open, which I do, I can hear the weather. I sank deeper into the warm water, watched the dark, and listened to it pour.

When I got out, I went straight to bed. There was a novel I wanted to finish, and a few bills to pay, but I just kept the light off, opened the window and crawled under the quilt. Right away I saw Gem's hand with a knife.

I thought about what the papers were saying, but couldn't agree. Slitting someone's throat is a personal act. Nothing "senseless" or "random" about it. Easy enough to drop a bomb or shoot off a gun, but try laying a knife edge on live flesh and pressing. Her flesh on his flesh, her eyes on his. Warm, breathing flesh yielding under her hand. I wouldn't have thought it, wouldn't even have dreamed it, but then I lack daring, even in my dreams.

2

Gina's face woke me, though her lips were all that remained. Blood-red, they hung suspended from the void that had been her face, mouthing words I couldn't hear. I should have stayed with her, but couldn't, and once awake I was alone, her hanging lips just out of reach.

Psychic, I would think later, just a few days later. At the time I pressed the sleep button on my alarm and pulled my quilt closer around me. She's just bored, I told myself. *Bitey*, she called it. Gina didn't merely get restless, the way other people did. Her boredom gaped like a mouth inside her. She prowled the streets and lives around her looking for things to feed it.

I assumed she'd taken Polly's money. Fifty lousy dollars and not a prayer of pulling it off. Which was probably the thrill, though she'd deny any thrill. *I only take what's mine*, I could already hear her protest. *I'm no thief*, she would say, but she was.

She was stealing the first time I ever laid eyes on her. Ten A.M. in the lingerie department at Eaton's. I was rummaging through the clearance bin of cotton underpants. She was directly in front of me, among the Lily of France lace panties, wearing black tights and a black leather vest with nothing but white skin underneath. Around her neck was a leather and chrome choker. I watched as she moved over to Christian Dior and stopped by a rack of delicate bras.

I admired how she stood: one hand on her hip, one hand on her chin, *considering*—as if she wasn't sure Christian Dior was quite high enough quality for boobs as fine as hers. She felt the fabric of one bra between her thumb and index finger, rejected it, then took another off its hanger. She pressed it to her cheek, her lips, then unzipped her vest and moulded the black lacy cup to her naked breast. Pale lips pursed, she turned in front of the mirror, watching herself from as many angles as possible. I watched, too, as she removed her fingers from the bra, raised her arms and folded her hands behind her head. In one unbroken move, she turned to her left, then to her right, arched deeply and snapped back up. The black lace clung to her skin. Satisfied, she removed it from her breast, folded it in two, dropped it into her bag, and zipped up her vest.

"Excuse me," I heard the saleswoman say as she moved into Maidenform.

"Yes?" She lifted her chin as if it were a weapon. The saleswoman took a step back, but persisted.

"May I see your bag?"

"What for?"

"I think you have some of our merchandise in it."

"Do you mean this?" She reached into her bag, pulled out the bra, and held it dangling in the saleswoman's face.

The saleswoman took another step back and said she was going to call security.

"Be my guest." As if the saleswoman was asking her permission. "I'll simply tell him I had every intention of making a purchase until you accused me of stealing."

"You had no intention of making a purchase," the saleswoman countered. "Why would you have . . . ?"

But Gina wasn't interested in the turn the conversation was taking.

"I'm a model, you know."

"I don't care what you are."

"You should be paying me to wear this bra. If I wore it for my show tonight, by 9:00 A.M. tomorrow this place would be crawling with men wanting to buy it for their wives and girlfriends. You wouldn't be able to keep it in stock." She tossed her head as if she had long hair she was trying to flip off her face, and as she did, she saw me watching. Her pale cheeks filled with colour, and her mouth, which at first had seemed too large, took her whole face with it when it curled into a smile. "I'm no thief," she said to me, and she tossed the bra at the saleswoman as she sauntered out of the store.

"Takes all kinds," the saleswoman said to me, mistaking me for one of her own. She picked the bra up from the floor, refolded it and placed it on the counter beside the cash register. I turned my eyes back to the clearance bin and chose three pairs of pink cotton hiphuggers and three striped bikinis.

"Are you a member of our Panty Club?" the saleswoman asked when I went up to pay.

"Your Panty Club?" What I wanted was the black lace bra. It lay deceitfully still, folded beside the cash. I had put on a bra absent-mindedly every day for years, never guessing the possibilities. I wanted to mould this one to my own breast the way she had, to feel it girding the tediousness of my life, infusing me with memories of experiences I hadn't even known I'd had. I wanted for my own the feeling I'd had watching her, the nerve-waking possibility of following something—my own life, even—to its furthest reaches. I couldn't remember the last time I had wanted anything so much. I felt dangerously alive.

"Buy eleven and the twelfth pair is free," the saleswoman said, punching six holes in my new card.

I smiled, thanked her, and put the card in my wallet between my driver's license and library card. When the saleswoman turned her back, I slipped the bra into my bag. I started walking slowly toward the exit, stopping to look at some nighties, as if I wasn't in any particular hurry to make it out the door. As I approached the exit, it occurred to me that the bra might be rigged with some sort of tracking device. Some sort of loud, ringing tracking device. I stopped walking and reached into my bag. I wanted it even more now, the edging of lace against my skin, the private journey to the edge of things as I folded laundry, made change and handed out soap. It seemed that only the exit stood between me and my desire. Once outside, I could bolt. No one would catch me, I was sure. But not completely sure. I slipped the bra back out of my bag and dropped it onto the floor near the exit.

The next time I saw Gina she had a cup of coffee on the table before her and a cigarette in her hand. This was at George's a few weeks later. I walked in before work and saw her right away, sitting in the booth by the window, looking out. She was in jeans and a T-shirt. With the same leather and chrome around her neck. Her eyes were clearer than I'd remembered. Bluer. Her hair darker, shorter. I didn't smile or nod at her as I took my stool at the counter. I assumed she didn't remember me. I didn't watch her smoke her cigarette or drink her coffee—nothing about her invited a lingering glance this time. I ordered my pie and coffee and left her alone.

One morning she was up at the counter talking to George when I came in.

"How old was she?" George was asking.

She shrugged. "Eighteen, I guess. Aren't we all?"

I looked at the skin around her eyes. Thin. Not quite papery.

Just beginning to map her pleasures and disappointments. Thirty, I guessed. My age. Give or take.

"Sixteen tops," she said after a moment. "And that's being generous to Roger."

George shook his head. "What does he think he's doing?"

"Roger doesn't think. Roger sees young tits, his eyes go tilt and his mouth goes, 'You're hired.' "

George filled my cup, and piled a few creams beside it. "Good morning," he said.

She turned to me. "Ah, the voyeur has arrived."

George's eyebrows shot up, but he didn't say a word. He hovered closer than he had to while he cut my wedge of pie.

"Been to any more private shows?" she asked me.

I tried to think of a reply, something to redeem myself—as if I was the one who needed redeeming—but couldn't. "No," I said, and sipped my coffee.

"I'm no thief, you know."

"I never said you were."

"But you thought it."

"Actually, I wasn't thinking that at all," I said, and smiled in what I hoped was a neutral way.

"I only take what's mine."

I nodded, still smiling, but in the pit of my stomach was the same feeling I'd had up in Lingerie. I looked at the woman leaning close enough for me to smell the mix of smoke and other things that clung to her, and remembered.

"And anyway, the law isn't made for people like us."

"Actually, it is," I said, not knowing yet how we were alike. "It's just not made *by* people like us."

She rewarded me with her full-faced smile. I thought she might say something shocking, or ask me my name.

"I'll remember that," she said. "Maybe when the cops come asking for my full *assistance* in their investigation." She said "assistance" as if she were spitting. "What do you think, George?" she asked, and I wondered when she and George got so tight.

"What's going on?" I asked, speaking into the air between her and George.

"Another kid is missing," George said.

I hadn't heard about it yet.

"Someone you know?" I asked her. I heard the tremor in my voice.

"Vaguely. She worked with me. I didn't really know her."

A practiced answer. I could imagine her giving it to the police, with the same tone and inflection. And to the press—if they decided to pick this one up and start asking their questions wherever it was she worked.

"Where do you work?"

"Xandu's."

I tried to place it.

"It's the one with the flashing tits in the window."

"The neon dancer?"

She nodded.

Just the nipples flashed. And the sign promising live girls.

"How long has she been missing?"

"Three days. She hasn't been to work for three days. Her roommate says she hasn't been home in four."

"What was her name?" I noticed I spoke in the past tense. She may have too.

"Teresa Marie," she said. She knew her more than vaguely.

I didn't say anything, and she didn't either. She played with one of her empty cream containers. George came by to refill our coffee. "That's OK," she said to him. "I should get going. I need to catch some sleep." She folded her hands together and rested her cheek against them, pantomiming sleep the way a four-year-old might.

"What's your name?" I asked.

"Gina."

"I'm Tova."

She scanned my face. "You don't look Danish."

"I'm not."

"So what are you doing with a Danish name?"

"It's not Danish."

"I worked with a girl named Tova once. She was Danish."

"It's also Hebrew," I said. "It means good."

"Good," she repeated, curling her lip. I wondered how it had ever escaped my notice what a ridiculous name I had. "I knew a girl named Joy once," Gina said.

I waited.

"She slit her wrists."

"That's good to know."

Gina smiled more fully. "It's OK," she said, reaching across her place setting to touch the back of my hand with her fingertips. The same fingertips that had held the black lace to her breast. Each finger had a silver ring encircling it, even her thumb. Some were linked with thin silver chains. Why her, I wondered as I fell freely inside myself. "Tova's not as bad as Joy," she said. "The very worst that can happen is that you'll be very bad." She was still smiling. "And that may not be such a bad thing."

She removed her chained fingers just as I was going to shake them off. She stopped smiling, and I saw how tired she was.

"I'll get your coffee," I said.

She nodded slowly, as if I had come up with something so unusual that it was taking some time to sink in. "That would be nice," she said. "That would be very nice."

They never found Teresa Marie. Not one piece of her. They found the next one, though. Wendy. No one Gina knew, even vaguely. The press gave her two paragraphs.

"Remains of Prostitute Found," Gina read to me. We were at the Ovaltine at the end of my day, the beginning of hers. Her choice, the Ovaltine. I'd argued for George's because of the booth by the window, but Gina had held her ground. She said the Ovaltine gave her a sense of history. I wasn't sure what kind, or whose, but because of it I was enduring wooden booths with no view of the street. "They don't even call her a woman. As if they would ever say 'Remains of John Found.' "

"Where'd they find her?"

"They don't say exactly. On the East Side. Like specifics aren't important east of Main."

"Probably the police don't want too much in the paper right now."

Gina looked up to flare her nostrils at me.

"Ah, Native," she said, looking down at the paper again. "*And* a prostitute. Well, that definitely explains it."

"What do you expect from the *Sun*?" I asked.

"Acknowledgement," she said, so simply that I thought, just for a second, that maybe it was.

Above me, the flat-footed thump of 4-C headed for the shower. Too late, I bolted up, then sank back. The chance for my share of the morning hot water was gone. Six thirty-eight and the first missed opportunity of the day was already behind me. The pipes in the walls and ceiling clanged, sending jets of hot water down 4-C's neck and back, filling his bathroom with steam. I pushed back my quilt, sat up and looked out the window for signs of daylight. Nothing but Vancouver's lights reflecting off the low sky.

I got up, put water on, then realized I was out of coffee. There were two boxes of herbal tea, though, two boxes more than I was likely to go through in this lifetime. Gina had brought them the second time she came for dinner. The first time, she'd brought flowers. Blue-and-purple irises. She'd stood in the hallway, held them out to me, then announced that she was on the first day of a three-day fast.

"I probably should have called to tell you. You didn't cook anything special, did you? Don't tell me."

"Come in," I said, took the flowers from her and led her toward the kitchen.

"You just go ahead and eat," Gina said as I arranged the flowers in a vase. "I'll have tea. Do you have ginseng tea?"

"I have some green tea."

She shook her head. "Can't do caffeine."

"How about apple cider?"

Gina shook her head again. "How about lemons? You have any organic lemons?"

"I have lemons."

"Conventionally grown?"

I didn't know what was conventional for lemons.

"I'll just have a glass of hot water, then. No, on second thought, I will have some lemon squeezed in. I can make it."

"It's OK. I can make it."

She watched as I moved the onions, mushrooms and eggplant off the cutting board, put it all in the fridge, and took out a lone lemon.

"You're not mad at me, are you?"

"No."

"You could be. I mean, I know I should have called and told you, made it for another night. You didn't cook anything special, did you?"

I looked at her and saw she was hoping I had.

"It's OK. I can eat it the rest of the week. I'm really not mad." I wasn't. I was strangely glad to have her in my kitchen and was only worried I wouldn't make her drink the way she liked it. I squeezed two tablespoons of lemon juice into the glass and poured hot water over it. "Honey?" I asked. She shook her head.

"My Aunt Belle used to swear by these," she told me as I handed her the glass. "She used to drink one every morning and every night. She said it flushed out her system and that was why she had the smoothest skin of all her sisters."

"Oh yeah? How's her skin now?"

"Well . . . she's dead now."

"Well . . . how was her skin before she died?"

Gina smiled. "Good. Really good."

I made myself a cup of tea and sat down at the table with her.

"Aren't you going to eat?" she asked.

"I'll eat later. I don't want to tempt you."

She smiled. "You don't?"

I didn't like the suggestion in her smile or the shift in her tone as she said that. It felt impersonal, practiced, disconnected from the awkward conversation we'd been having. "No," I said, and busied myself with my tea bag.

She reached across the table to touch my arm. "It's OK," she said.

"What's OK?" I asked and saw she was sweating. "Are you all right?" She looked too pale to be embarking on a fast; her eyes were too bright.

She removed her hand from my arm and wiped her face. "Yeah. It's just all the poison seeping out."

"What poison?"

"Just all the shit that accumulates from eating poisoned food and drinking poisoned water day after day. It happens whenever I fast." She met my eye. I didn't say anything. "I don't do drugs."

"I didn't say you did."

"But you thought it."

"How would you know what I was thinking?"

"I'm not stupid."

"You're not a mind reader either."

She got up from the table, went over to the sink, removed her choker and washed her face and neck.

"Do you always wear that?"

She sat back down at the table, blew on the chrome and rubbed it clean against her shirt. "You think I'm into weird shit, don't you?" She took a sip of her hot lemon and grimaced. "You hope I am, anyway."

"Oh please," I said, ashamed to feel my colour rising. "Why don't we just sit here the rest of the night and you can tell me what I think and hope."

"I'm sorry," she said and made an attempt at a smile. I didn't think "sorry" was a word she used much. Her mouth looked like it might break on the word.

"You accuse *me* of voyeurism," I said, "but if I try to have a normal conversation with you, you won't. You have to turn everything into some kind of a peep-show."

I thought I might have gone too far, but when I looked at her face she was still attempting a smile.

"Why don't you tell me what you were thinking?" she said.

"I was just wondering why you always wear a choker." A thick choker, heavy around her neck. "It looks like it would be uncomfortable."

"It's not uncomfortable. Not too, anyway." She smiled. "I wear it as a reminder."

"Of what?"

"It's not mine," she said and ran her finger along one of its edges. "It belonged to Terry. Teresa Marie." She met my eye to make sure I remembered who that was, saw that I did, and shifted away. "She lent it to me for a show I was doing."

"What kind of show?"

"Oh, just a leather-and-lace routine. Nothing too daring." She smiled again. "Xandu's isn't in the business of stretching imaginations." I thought maybe I should smile too, but wasn't sure. "Anyway, Terry lent it to me, just for the couple of weeks I was doing that one routine."

I wondered if a black lace bra was part of that routine.

"So now I'm just waiting for when I can give it back to her." She pulled it away from her neck. "I actually hate wearing it. And it's beginning to smell."

I tried to think of something to say, something to change the expression on her face, but couldn't, so I poured some more hot water into her glass.

.

"To go," I said to George when I finally made it to his place at 7:15 that morning, a half-hour behind schedule.

"Where's the fire?"

"I'm late."

"So you'll open at 7:35," he said, but he was already pouring my coffee into styrofoam. "Apple or blackberry?"

"Apple," I said, then reconsidered. "Maybe a bit of both."

George gave no indication of having heard me but he took out both pies.

"Gina been in?" I asked.

"This morning?"

I knew she hadn't. The only time she made it to George's before noon was if she was still up from the night before. She was not a morning person. Yet another reason she hated her new job.

"I'm just not the retail type," she had said soon after she started at Polly's. I would have thought she'd have been relieved to find a job so soon after being fired from Xandu's. Thankful. "It's the routine of it," she said. "The cunt-numbing routine."

If you worried less about your cunt, I wanted to say, but wasn't sure how to finish the sentence . . . *you too could manage a laundromat?* Somehow, it didn't seem compelling.

Then it was the customers: rude, boring and perverted. "They think I don't know what they're planning to do with those hamsters they're buying."

"What do you mean? What do you think they're planning to do?"

"Don't you know about hamsters?"

"They're just buying them for pets, Gina."

"Where have you been living, girl?" she asked, and wouldn't admit she was trying to pull my leg.

Then it was Polly, at first a simple half-cunt, then a full-fledged slave dealer. "And to think it's legal," Gina said one day, as I was trying to get through a backlog of drop-offs.

"And to think what's legal?" I asked.

"Imprisoning innocent animals and selling them to whoever wants to buy. I mean, do we know anything about our customers, or what they're planning to do with the animals? No. And does Polly care? Of course not. All she cares about is counting her filthy bills at the end of the day."

27

I assumed she was kidding, but her face was serious.

"The same could be said about Roger, you know."

She didn't answer right away, didn't indicate that she had heard what I'd said. She plunged into the pile of clothes I'd just pulled from a dryer and started folding. She had the moves. Faster than me, more precise, better. "Roger pays his girls," she said after a while. "I don't see Polly slipping a ten to any of her goldfish. And everyone working for Roger is there by her own choice. No one's forcing anyone to swing her tits. Every single girl at Xandu's can walk out the door any time she chooses."

"Hey." George was snapping his fingers too close to my face. "What planet are you on today anyway?" He was holding out the bag with my pie and coffee.

"I'm a bit off," I admitted, then noticed the change. "You're growing a beard," I blurted.

"Trying to." His hand shot up to cover a bare patch in the middle of the scraggly growth. "It's just the second day."

"It looks good," I lied—I think because I had never seen him sheepish before. And because somewhere inside myself I appreciated—envied—that he cared how he looked. Enough to stand in front of the mirror and wish himself more handsome, more attractive, and then try to do something about it. I looked down at the grubby-looking jeans I'd worn every day that week, then back at him and repeated, "It looks good. It just needs a bit of time. It'll grow in."

He removed his hand from the offending bare patch and looked at himself in the mirror behind the counter. I could remember looking at myself that appreciatively in the mirror once, and wondered if I ever would again. "You really think so?" he asked.

"Yeah. Yeah, I do." I was beginning to believe it. With his crooked half-smile, under the right lighting and the right set of eyes, the scraggliness could pass for ruggedness. "If you see Gina, would you tell her to come by the laundromat?" I wanted to see more than the disembodied lips of my dream.

"Sure thing," George said, pulling himself away from the mirror. I risked a quick glance at myself and saw how it was.

I didn't always look like hell, I decided as I looked in the mirror at work. My skin, always sallow this time of year, looked almost yellow under the fluorescent light of the laundromat, but with a bit of blood rushing under it, a bit of life in my eyes . . .

"Got a smoke?" Josie interrupted.

"Uh uh." I shook my head. As I poured her morning mug of coffee, Josie twisted her mouth in anticipation of my next line. *Don't start with me, Jose. You know you can't smoke in here.* That's what I usually said. I knew I should say it now. Then she could get mad at me, huddle closer to the radiator and drink her coffee while I counted the till and checked the machines. *Don't start with me . . .* It was what we did together, had been doing together every morning going on four years now. It formed part of the foundation of our day. "Uh uh," I repeated and went back behind the counter.

It wasn't actually hell I resembled, I decided. Hell burned, I didn't even flicker. Two years since Lynn had left and only the occasional stirring. Nothing that would inspire anything as dramatic as George's attempt to grow a beard. Nothing that anyone would recognize as a sign of continuing life within. Though Gina had.

"Want to talk about it?" she'd asked me soon after our non-dinner at my house. I was over at her place late in the afternoon.

"Talk about what?" It was my first time in her apartment and I

29

was trying to decide if I liked it. She had the turret of the house—an old Victorian—and had painted her domed ceiling gold. Shiny once, possibly, it had tarnished to a dullness as oppressive as the grey that pressed up against her windows.

"Your crush on me," she said, smiling broadly.

"What crush on you?" I asked, adding "Don't flatter yourself" too late to have the intended effect.

"I'm straight, you know."

I must have raised my eyebrows, because she giggled and said, "Really. I am."

"What do you mean by straight?"

"I mean I like to fuck men." She smiled again. "So what about your crush on me?"

"What about it?"

"I don't want to lead you on."

I laughed. Meant to, at least.

"I mean, I'm not saying I *never* sleep with women, but as a general rule—"

"You really don't have to keep going at this," I interrupted, and to my surprise found myself talking about Lynn.

"Eight years. Jesus," Gina said when I'd finished talking. "I didn't even live with my parents that long."

"You didn't?"

She shook her head. I didn't ask her what had happened—mostly because she hadn't asked me what had happened to split me from Lynn. I'd liked that. She'd just listened and nodded as if she knew that the causes of these things can't be explained or understood. At least that's what I'd been telling myself ever since I realized I would never really understand it. It was what you did next that mattered, I told myself. Or didn't do, as in my case. Which was the problem. Which was why my crush on Gina—or whatever it was—really didn't matter. Why nothing I felt mattered. I got the feeling that Gina understood.

"How long has it been?" she asked.

I told her. I liked that she didn't say I would be over it soon, or that it was time to move on. She just nodded again, as if she knew something she wasn't saying out loud.

Now a year had passed since that conversation. Long enough for even me to acknowledge that my inability to do anything "next" had little to do with Lynn. I wondered if that was what Gina had been thinking. Or if she had known how much I'd initially hoped she might be the igniting spark. I dialled her number. No answer.

As I put the phone down I saw Josie rummaging through her purse looking for cigarettes, a blank look on her face. I knew she had no cigarettes. I knew I should tell her she couldn't smoke in here anyway. She relied on me for it.

The first customer came in. He needed change and soap. Josie was still rummaging when he finished loading and turned the machine on.

"Got a smoke?" she asked him.

"Sorry." He smiled.

Josie went back to her rummaging, piling some of the contents of her bag onto the floor beside her. Bits of twine, newspaper clippings, several paintbrushes of different sizes, more matches than I would have thought possible—this a woman always asking for a light—and cigarettes. Packs of them. I began to feel uneasy. Just because I had decided I needed a change didn't mean Josie had.

"C'mon Jose," I called from the counter, hoping it wasn't too late, not sure what I was afraid might happen. "You know you can't smoke in here."

She looked at me, anger beginning to fill in her emptiness. Reassured, I repeated what I had said. She glared at me and huddled closer to the radiator. I watched her start drinking her coffee and realized how tired I was of her and her stupid rituals. Her stupid rituals which had now become mine. She felt my stare and returned it until I turned away and started recounting the till.

Two more customers came in. I gave them change, then dialled Gina. This time she answered.

"Gina?"

"No, Madonna."

At the sound of her voice I could see her face again clearly.

"Did you call just to breathe heavily into the phone?" she asked.

"I was wondering if you wanted to have dinner tonight."

"You're calling me at 7:45 in the morning to ask me about dinner tonight?"

"No. I'm calling you because I had a weird dream about you and wanted to make sure you're OK."

"Weird how?"

I didn't want to tell her. "I don't remember it all. All I could see was your mouth."

"That's because you'd like me to eat you."

"Fuck you."

"You wish," I heard her say before I slammed down the phone.

"Bitch," I said. One of my customers looked up for a moment. Josie muttered "Filthy girl" as she piled her belongings back into her bag.

"It's OK, Josie," I said.

But Josie refused to be reassured. She continued rearranging her belongings. I watched her and wondered if she even knew what OK meant, if Gina knew, if either of them had ever spent so much as a minute in that bland territory so familiar to me. Josie muttered something I didn't catch.

"It's OK, Jose," I started to say again, then stopped, wondering when I'd relinquished my claim to anything more.

3

I took the bus ome. A mistake, and not only because my legs ached for the release of a long walk after work. It was the ad in the bus shelter, the well-muscled young woman staring insolently at me from a locker-room bench. Accusingly. *Just do it*, she commanded, her full lips sullenly parted. *Just do what?* I wanted to ask back, but I knew what she meant, and it wasn't folding clothes and handing out change day after day, or scurrying to and from work under the cover of darkness like some oversized mole. She meant IT—I knew about IT—and despite myself, I could feel my cramped legs stretching out, finding their pace, carrying me lightly, effortlessly; sweat, worry, loneliness pouring freely off me as I crested mountains, lifted off . . .

I considered for a moment that Lynn might have put her up to it, then blushed at the pathetic wish in that thought, the impossible hope that from a distance of three years and a whole new life Lynn would have any interest in continuing an argument we had already exhausted by the time she decided to leave me. "Go to hell," I said to the model. She stared back at me, unfazed. She'd met my type before. We spent lifetimes daydreaming different lives for ourselves while she just did it, grabbed it, reached for her own. "I'm probably happier than she is anyway," I said to myself as the bus pulled up to the curb. I didn't look back as I boarded. I had already watched one woman like her shrug, get up and walk away.

I had planned to settle into an empty seat, lean against the window and read—I was halfway through a mystery and was beginning to care who'd done it—but it was 5:45, the end of the workday. There was barely an empty bit of floor to stand on, just a lot of wet coats and tired breath packed together for the evening ride home. I wedged myself among damp wool, reached for the railing above me and tried not to breathe too deeply.

The woman in the ad was probably finishing her preliminary stretches, maybe working out one last crick in her neck. By the time we crawled to the corner of Hastings and Clark she'd be doing it, IT, her breathing steady, eyes on the horizon. It was a lie to say I was probably happier than she was. I wasn't happy; I was OK. I had hoped my life would be more than OK.

I felt my left calf cramp and shifted my weight. As the cramp subsided, a low tide of relief surged through me. *It all comes down to balance,* I told myself. *Lulls are just a part of life, boredom's as necessary as excitement . . .* Clichés, I knew, commonplace, but what was so terrible about "commonplace"? When had "commonplace" become a code word for a failed life? That was something I had wondered ever since Lynn accused me of it, hurled the word at me as if she had finally hit on the perfect justification for leaving me.

"Why not just admit you've fallen in love with Amy?" I had countered. "You don't have to start making up reasons why you're better than me in order to leave."

"I'm not better than you," she'd replied, sidestepping Amy, the heat of a new lover, the thrill of seeing herself through new eyes after eight years under the familiar gaze of mine. "I just wish you would admit that you're in a rut, we're in a rut together. Just admit for once that you're bored stiff."

"I'm not bored," I protested, but knew it was useless. Lynn had always mistaken contentment for boredom.

"Well I am," she said.

"Boredom's vastly underrated," I responded, satisfied to see her cheeks flush with anger. I waited for her response. She shrugged, got up and walked out of the room.

The bus stopped just outside George's. I considered getting off, calling Gina, telling her I'd scored the booth by the window, to meet me there for supper, but then what? Gina and I seemed to spend more and more of our time bitching at each other while we sat around waiting for something to happen. And I had been looking forward to finishing my mystery, cleaning up a bit, maybe even cooking myself a regular meal. I wasn't willing to let a ridiculous ad throw my whole evening off. I got off at my own stop, picked up some vegetables and chocolate at the corner grocer and tried to ignore Lynn's voice still echoing in my mind. *Inflexible*, she was calling me now; *stuck in routine*. It occurred to me that it might take more than the mere passage of time to exorcise Lynn's parting voice.

The evening was ruined; still I persisted. I read my mystery compulsively from the moment I got home, only to feel manipulated by the slick inevitability of all the pieces falling into place. I made tea but pulled the bag too soon, ate a cheese sandwich then realized it was a green salad I'd been wanting, picked up the phone to call Gina then put it down again without dialling. I did fifty sit-ups, twenty push-ups, amazed at how much effort it took. Once strong, my muscles were now as underused as the rest of me. At midnight I went to bed, fell into a dreamless sleep, and woke up seven hours later with a stale mouth and an exhaustion that felt like a call for something other than rest.

When I got to work Josie was already waiting on the doorstep, ready for a repeat of the day before, and the day before that. I wondered how *she* spent the time in between.

"Hi Josie."

"It's raining."

"It's supposed to clear tomorrow," I said and waited for her to make a comment about her umbrella.

"Good I brought my umbrella," she said as I unlocked the door.

"Yes it is." I didn't ask if that was the one her brother had given her.

"My brother gave it to me."

The postman.

"He's a postie, you know."

"Uh huh," I said, fighting a new wave of exhaustion. I turned on the lights, hung up my coat and put water on for coffee. Josie took up her position by the radiator.

"Cops came by," Josie said.

"Here?" I asked quickly.

Josie shook her head. "Big fight at my place," she said.

I was disappointed, and realized I had actually been looking forward to their arrival, their questions, their careful consideration of my answers. *The Avenger*, I'd overheard someone call Gem—the police couldn't be liking that much—and I was someone who had known her. They were bound to wonder what I knew.

The water boiled and I poured it over the grounds. As the coffee bubbled up and released itself to the hot water I wondered if it was possible I actually did know something, some bit of information that Gem had revealed to me and to no one else. It seemed unlikely, but she had to have told someone something, and wasn't it always the unlikeliest characters who hold the clues? I recreated Gem's face in my mind, her pale-lashed eyes, her narrow mouth sipping at her coffee. I could hear her voice; my mind rushed to it, to the possibility that there was something I knew, some piece of the puzzle I, alone, inadvertently held.

I brought Josie her coffee as my thoughts reeled back, eight months back to when Gem first started coming to the laundromat. I remembered the photograph of the missing girl she had shown me, bits of conversations we'd had. I hadn't picked up anything unusual, certainly not anything murderous. Gem was earnest, grim even, but who wouldn't be, chasing after missing street kids day after day? I'd seen angrier, more outraged, more despairing women. If she harboured any passion at all behind her flat, round face, it seemed to be reserved for birds. She loved birds—more than kids, I suspected. I'd told her once that she reminded me of an owl, and she'd smiled openly, unreservedly delighted. "An owl?" Her narrow mouth fell open, suddenly loose and generous; her wide, yellow-brown eyes opened wider. I tried to explain what I meant, what it was about her face, but couldn't because her smile had cracked it, and her face unfrozen wasn't owl-like at all.

Josie grabbed the coffee from me with both hands, spilling a few drops.

"Careful," I said sharply, resentful at the intrusion.

Josie didn't seem to notice. "Cops came by," she said.

I ignored her as I tried to recall other conversations with Gem, clues she might have dropped.

"Big fight at my place," Josie's voice gnawed into my thoughts. There was nothing new or interesting in what she was saying, nothing to compel me to focus on her instead of Gem, except that she was the one sitting a few feet from me, dripping coffee all over the clean white surface of one of my dryers, staring at my face. Reluctantly, I stared back.

Josie's appeal, when we first met, was that she bore no resemblance to Joan of Arc. There had been a run of Joans frequenting my laundromat at that time. I don't know why—a late-night movie, maybe something on the news. It wasn't a trend I enjoyed. I was used to different personalities, famous or not, moving into any vacant or half-occupied bodies they could find around the neighbourhood, but Joan depressed me. More than that, she repelled me. It was her eyes, partly—too bright for the worn faces they burned out of. And her perverted sense of heroism. The moment she moved into customers of mine, whatever joy they'd once derived from the offerings of this world—coffee, tea, a good joke, the warmth of a radiator—drained right out of them. Ordinary pleasures suddenly became tests of sorts, temptations that, if yielded to, would only weaken their spirit for the battle ahead. And for what battle? What purpose? What about squeezing what you could out of the life you got? Wasn't that a worthy enough battle? Wasn't that heroic enough? *What's so great about being burned at the stake that you'll choose it over a mug of hot coffee?* I wondered.

"Doesn't it hurt?" I asked one of them when she came in one day with her arms freshly bandaged after her latest skirmish with the enemy. I had known her as Cassie long before she was Joan, had helped her fold her sheets once or twice. I felt I could ask her.

"Doesn't what hurt?"

"Your arms."

"My arms?"

"Your arms. Didn't you cut your arms?" Slashed them, is what she had done, as if they were confidential documents that had to be destroyed or altered beyond all recognition.

She looked at a spot above and behind my head where only Joan herself could see who hovered. "These aren't my arms."

Whose are they, then? I didn't ask. *Whose arms are they, then, you stupid wasteful woman, if not your own?* I knew stupidity had nothing to do with it, and that I wasn't necessarily the best or even a good judge of what was a waste of a life, a mind, a perfectly good set of arms, but Joan infuriated me. Surely there were other personalities . . . Cleopatra, for example, who at least could have added a touch of splendour to my laundromat. Or Isadora Duncan, whose dances might have transformed the long hours of the afternoon. Why did my laundromat have to attract a small herd of chapped-lipped Joans with their pinched faces and their eyes oddly lit in anticipation of their eventual immolation?

All of which is why I took to Josie. When she walked in off the street the anger in her glare had not so much as a hint of the transcendent. She smelled of cigarettes and unwashed body parts. Bits of old meals filled the spaces between her teeth. And when I offered her coffee, she grabbed the mug with two street-weathered hands. Her needs were of this world; we had that in common. I invited her to warm herself by the radiator.

At first she was a comfort to me. I saw her as a survivor, someone determined to hold on to the life she had, even if it was only her little rituals that kept her anchored in it, but soon I realized that her rituals were more than just an anchor. They had taken her over, replaced the life they were supposed to protect. Every day with her seemed to be a reenactment of everything that had safely transpired the day before, every conversation repeated, every cup of coffee drunk with the same motions and held with the same cradling hands.

I began to resent her, the stupid rituals that soon controlled my workday, the sameness that ruled my laundromat. At my worst moments, I saw myself in her. I would hear Lynn's voice—
inflexible, stuck in routine—and feel that my own daily routines had become the same sort of prison to me. I fantasized, now, about

shattering Josie's rules—maybe putting sugar in her coffee instead of cream—and sliding with her into the unknown.

"Are we still fighting?" Gina asked when she called a little later. Her voice sounded husky, like she was getting a cold or had spent the night smoking.

"We weren't fighting. You were being a bitch."

"Oh yeah." She inhaled deeply, as if she might actually offer some sort of explanation, then didn't. "How are things at the Kwik Kleen?" she asked.

I never referred to the laundromat by its name. It embarrassed me, made me feel that I, by association, was as stupid as the name.

"The same. Shitty. I realized this morning I'm so bored I'm actually looking forward to the cops coming by and questioning me."

"What are you talking about? What would they want to question you about?"

"Gem. Remember? Psycho sex slayer? Former customer of mine?"

"Oh Christ." She inhaled deeply again. On a cigarette, I realized. "I wouldn't waste my time worrying about that. Ten to one the cops don't even know you exist."

I knew she was wrong. They had to know I exist. Gem and I had talked, laughed together. What's more, we'd been *seen* talking and laughing together. The police were bound to wonder what I knew.

"Anyway, she didn't do it," Gina said.

"What do you mean, she didn't do it?"

"I mean she didn't do it."

"How do you know? You don't know anything, do you?" I asked.

"Don't be crazy," she said.

Maybe someone at the bar had heard something, I thought. One of the other dancers. *Fucking fleas*, Gina had called the police. *They're even hanging around the bar now.* Maybe Gina had heard something, knew something.

"Anyway," Gina was saying, "Lois told me that two girls quit last week so I spoke to Rog again. I get the feeling if I can drop ten pounds he'll take me back."

"Rog? You're calling him Rog now?"

"He's not that bad, Tova, really. At least he never accused me of stealing from his till."

"Speaking of which, how *is* Polly?"

"The same. Out, thank God. Her latest is that I'm not allowed to smoke at work." She inhaled again on her cigarette. "Like her precious hamsters and goldfish might come down with lung cancer or something."

"Did she ever find her missing fortune?"

There was a pause, then, "I didn't take her fucking money, Tova."

"Jesus, Gina. Relax. I didn't say you did."

"You didn't have to. Hold on a sec."

I waited while she rang up a sale, then, when she came back on, I asked why they had quit.

"Who?"

"The two girls."

"I don't know. I didn't ask Lois for their entire life stories."

"Well, maybe you should find out."

"What do you mean, find out?"

"I mean, it's been a couple of months since you worked there. You don't really know what's going on. If girls are suddenly quitting, right and left, I don't think you should go running back until you know why." I was surprised by my own calm. I felt competent and in charge of something—Gina's life, if not my own—for the first time that day.

"They're not *suddenly* quitting. There's always turnover at a place like Xandu's," Gina said in a tone that reminded me I knew nothing of her life and of the world she lived in when she wasn't visiting me in mine.

"Still . . ." I said, but already I felt deflated. I noticed a customer shaking a washer that wouldn't start. He was facing the machine, one hand on either side, and shaking it as hard as he could. I told Gina I had to get off the phone before he started kicking it.

"I can't believe you think I took Polly's money. Do you really think I would risk my neck for fifty lousy dollars?" she asked.

Yes, I wanted to say. *For less than fifty dollars.* "You've been known to do idiotic things," I said.

"Yeah, well, not this one."

"So what am I going to tell the cops when they come by?" I asked Josie a little later. She ignored me.

Gee officer, I don't know. I wasn't really her confidante. I do remember her getting a bit irked about all those girls going missing and you fellows saying something about your hands being tied. Oh? Were his hands tied behind his back? Or maybe I could fill them in about crucial personal information. Case-breaking information I alone possessed. *She loved birds*, I could enlighten them. *Hawks and eagles especially. Owls most of all.*

I realized Josie was staring at me. Her blue eyes were clearer than I'd ever seen them. I wondered, for the first time, if she'd been handsome as a girl. "Always tell the truth," she said before fading out again. She cradled her empty coffee mug in her hands as her upper lip started rubbing against the lower. I brought her more coffee, just to give her something else to do with her mouth. I couldn't stand the thought of watching her spend the rest of the morning doing nothing but work her lips against each other.

4

Had Gina disappeared when I was fifteen I might have been prepared. That was the year I read *Lord Jim* and was sharp with his notion that every person is granted one opportunity in life to prove himself a hero. Or to fail completely. It was the fairness of the prospect that drew me—an equal-opportunity type of heroism that even I could lay claim to—and its all-or-nothing simplicity. All I had to do, it seemed, all I would ever have to do, was recognize my moment and seize it. I waited for wars to break out around me, for buildings to explode, for mountains to spew fire and lava, so I could dive into the horror and prove myself, once and forever.

By thirty-two, though, I was no longer watching for that sort of thing. I was too busy getting through moments to think about how I might seize them, too challenged by the day-to-day to worry about the once-in-a-lifetime. I had traded in my adrenalin for endurance and had stopped scanning the far horizons of my life. I was completely unprepared.

So unwatchful had I become that for several days I didn't even fully realize she was gone.

"Have you seen Gina around?" I asked George the evening of that first day.

"Today?"

"Yeah. She was supposed to meet me here at six."

George glanced at the clock on the mirrored wall behind the counter. It was already seven. "Looks like you got stood up," he said, and when I didn't smile, he asked if I had tried calling her.

"She's not home."

"Did you have a fight?" he asked.

"No. No more than usual."

George smiled. "Seems like lately I can't even pour her a cup of coffee without her jumping down my neck about something."

"The eggs *were* a bit rubbery that day, George," I said, though it's true Gina shouldn't have gotten so worked up over it.

George shrugged. "You order them over-medium, I can't be held responsible for what happens. They're meant to be cooked over-easy or hard-boiled. Anything in between and the texture goes off."

I nodded, sparing him the information that Gina cooked perfect eggs over-medium.

"Something's eating her," George went on. "The other morning—what's today, Wednesday?"

I nodded.

"So, Monday, I think; it was after you left for work. She came in—looking like hell, I might add—and right away started up with a couple of girls who were sitting at the counter."

"What do you mean, 'started up'? What were they doing?"

"Nothing. Minding their own business."

I found that hard to believe. "Did she know them?"

George smiled. "She didn't have to. She could smell them."

"What do you mean?"

"Undercover cops."

I rolled my eyes. George thought everyone was an undercover cop.

"It wasn't like her," George went on. "They weren't bothering her. They weren't even looking at her. I swear, you would think she was paranoid or something the way she asked them what they thought they were looking at."

"What *were* they looking at?"

George shrugged. "Beats me. Not her. Their coffee, maybe. She's just gotten touchy as hell."

I creamed and sugared my coffee while we both thought for a moment about what a bitch Gina had become.

"I think it's that new job of hers," George decided. "She's not the type of girl to be hidden away behind a cash register all day."

"She's not a girl," I said.

"She needs an audience, a bit of excitement," George said, ignoring me.

"Oh please," I said. It went against something in me to admit to George—to any man—that Gina might have been happier stripping every night for a roomful of sleazy men than she was selling hamsters and birds at a perfectly nice pet store. "She just misses the adrenalin rush. She'll get used to it."

George raised his eyebrows. "Not everybody does, you know."

Something that flared in his eyes at that moment—it was brief, gone before it could spread to his face—made me wonder how he had ever landed himself behind a counter, feeding people like me all day, every day.

"Anyway, Roger's a complete scumbag," I said. "Gina's lucky he fired her."

George thought about that, then replied, "Maybe so. Or maybe not."

I waited for him to go on.

"So, are you going to eat anything?" he asked.

"I'm still deciding," I said, suddenly famished. I realized I hadn't eaten anything since my pie and ice cream before work. Coffee, sugar and fat spurred me through my days. And endurance. No wonder I was exhausted.

"How about a sandwich?" George asked.

"That sounds good. Maybe a tuna on rye, but hold the—"

"I know, I know," he said, putting both hands up in front of him. "Hold the everything."

"Right."

"Hold the flavour," I heard him mutter as he went to make it and fill a few other orders. When he brought my sandwich, he had added a green salad and a heap of fries. I asked him if he'd heard anything about anything.

"Anything about anything," he repeated.

"You know. About Gem. Or that guy in the dumpster."

"What's to hear?" he asked. "Gem, as you call her, is gone. And the guy in the dumpster is dead."

"What do you mean, as I call her?"

"The woman the cops are looking for is called Jewel. Jewel Ann Bonin."

"How do you know?" I asked, trying not to slobber ketchup all over my chin as I ate my fries.

"How do you like the fries?" he asked.

"Fine. They're great," I said, anxious to get back to Gem.

"Do you find they're a bit crisper on the outside?"

"Maybe a little."

George beamed. "I added a bit of beef fat to the oil," he said. "Just a touch. It fries everything up a little crisper and adds a nice flavour."

"Delicious," I assured him, and ate another few fries in as attentive a manner as I could. Then I asked again how he knew about Gem's "real" name.

"I pick things up," he said.

"Come on, George." I didn't mind his attempts at discretion

when we were exchanging neighbourhood gossip, but this was different. "This is serious," I said, at which point he leaned right over the counter, across my place setting, to bring his face to mine. I could smell the last cigarette he'd smoked. "I'm the one who knows that," he said.

"What do you mean, you're the one who knows that?"

"You're the one who seems to think this is all some kind of game," he said, getting out of my face before I had to tell him to. *"Amazon Avenger."* He practically spit the words at me.

"Jesus, George. Relax." I tried to remember who I'd been talking to when I came up with that one. "I didn't realize you made a habit of eavesdropping on your customers' conversations."

George shook his head. "Let me tell you something," he said. He was obviously going to tell me whether I let him or not. "There's a solid line between dreaming about offing some prick and actually doing it."

"Why'd you call him a prick?" I asked, but George waved me quiet.

"And people like you and me can't even begin to imagine what's on the other side of that line."

I waited a bit to show I was letting the full impact of his words sink in, then said, "So you also think he was a prick."

"I know he was a prick," George said, standing up straight again and pressing both his palms into his lower back. I wondered if his disk was hurting him again. "That's not the point."

"I got your point, all right? Just tell me how you know he's a prick."

"Was," George corrected. "Everyone knows."

"What do you mean, everyone knows? I don't know."

"Well now you do. He was a regular around here. Everyone knew him."

I waited.

"He liked young girls."

I nodded, not sure why that would have made him any more of a prick than all the others I saw cruising kids on the streets.

"He played a bit rough," George added, dropping his voice as if he was the one who should be ashamed.

"What do you mean, 'played'? You mean he beat them up?"

"Basically."

"After he fucked them or during?" I asked.

George shrugged. Usually he would have told me to watch my language. Usually I wouldn't have used that language with George. He went over to the grill, threw on a few burgers, flipped a couple that had been sitting there—for too long, I suspected—and started filling orders.

"How much you want to bet girls stop mysteriously disappearing now?" I called out to him. My voice sounded weird, too loud, but for once I didn't care that everyone in the place could hear me. They knew the score as well as I did anyway: eight dead at last count, several more still missing, and the cops scratching their heads the whole time, urging women to "be cautious," whatever that was supposed to mean. Gem had obviously figured out what the cops couldn't seem to piece together. Couldn't be bothered to piece together.

George walked back over to me shaking his head. "He was a prick, not a killer."

"How do you know?"

George hesitated, then said, "Because they found another girl this morning."

I felt my mouth go dry.

"Where?"

"New Brighton."

"How do you know?" I hadn't seen anything in the *Province* or the *Sun*.

"A couple of girls she used to work with . . ."

"Did you know her?" I asked.

He hesitated. "She came in from time to time."

"What was her name?"

George screwed his mouth up as if he had to think really hard. "I don't know," he said.

"Two of your customers were talking about a friend of theirs who got murdered and her name didn't come up?"

"Sally, I think."

"Sally," I repeated dully.

"Look," George said, suddenly weary of the conversation, or of me. "I don't know how we got onto that. I probably shouldn't have said anything. It'll be in the papers tomorrow anyway. All I was trying to get through to you is that whatever is going on . . ." He paused. "This Gem isn't someone you should be looking for. You shouldn't be sticking your nose into any of this stuff, sniffing around like . . ."

I knew he wanted to say "like a bitch in heat." It was a favourite expression of his, though he hadn't applied it to me yet.

". . . like this is exciting or something," he finished. "You want excitement, go sky diving."

"I'm afraid of heights."

George didn't smile.

"I wasn't looking for her. All I did was ask if you'd heard anything more. I was just trying to have a simple conversation with you." George still wasn't smiling. "Why would you think I'm looking for her?" I asked.

He looked at me as if he wasn't sure he should go ahead. "Because Gina is."

"She is?"

"Yeah. Yeah, she is."

I was stunned.

"Gina doesn't even know her, hardly. She was *my* customer," I said. "Why would Gina be looking for her?"

George shrugged. "Beats me. Gina lives in a fantasy world," he said, leaving me stung, confused. What did George know about Gina's fantasy world? I didn't ask. I was suddenly afraid of the answer. I hadn't considered before that I might be competing with George for Gina's confidence. For Gina. I looked at him to see if I could detect the beginnings of one-upmanship. He was motioning to a customer that he would be over in a moment to take her order.

"Who are you growing your beard for?" I asked.

He laughed. "The things you think of," he said, but didn't answer my question.

"I sincerely doubt that Gina's looking for Gem. I just spoke to her this morning," I added. "She told me to meet her here at six."

George raised his eyebrows, but said nothing as he stacked my dishes.

"And neither of us really needs your advice on this. We're both quite capable of taking care of ourselves."

George cocked his head and looked at me sideways.

"Why are you mad? " he asked.

"I'm not mad," I lied, and left a large tip to prove he was wrong.

There was no identifiable moment which divided my knowing she was gone from my not knowing, no event, conversation or middle-of-the-night premonition which thrust me into knowledge, let alone action. I believe in epiphanies, but they don't happen to me. I'm a slow-seepage sort of person, more like a poorly built basement than a weather vane.

She's done this before, I reassured myself, as I dialled her number and listened to it ring. *Laying low,* she called it when she unplugged her phone and slept for days. The first few times she did it, I thought something must have happened at the bar—a customer had threatened her, was stalking her, even, but when I asked her she laughed and said, "Nothing that exotic." As if the sexual safaris some men went on were exotic and being their prey just another sort of adventure. "It's hard to explain," she added, then tried. "Sometimes I just feel strange, though nothing strange is going down." When I said nothing, asked nothing more, she shrugged and smiled. "Nothing to do but sleep it off, I guess," she said, which was what I assumed she was doing now. Although until now she had always warned me beforehand.

I tried calling her at work, only to be told what I already knew.

"Gina's not in," a high, young voice informed me on the second day. Thursday.

"Is that Polly?" I asked on the third.

"Polly stepped out for a sec. Who's this?" she asked.

I told her I was a friend of Gina's, and asked if she knew when Gina might be in, where I might reach her.

If you're such a friend, why wouldn't she tell you herself? I half expected to be challenged. "I don't know," she said instead. "I'm just filling in." A pause, then she half whispered, excited, confiding: "Actually, Polly just asked me on full-time, permanent."

I almost congratulated her. It's an automatic response with me, seeing only half the situation. Someone was offered a job, congratulations were in order. So what if I didn't know her? So what if the job she was offered belonged to a friend of mine, a friend who was obviously missing, even if I hadn't quite managed to acknowledge it?

"When did she ask you?"

"Just this morning."

Why? I might have asked. *Did Gina call, offer her resignation?*

I thanked her for her time, asked her to have Polly call me, then neglected to leave my number.

Even if I had realized then that Gina was missing, what would I have done? What, realistically, could I have done? It was Friday, always a busy day, everybody concluding, all at the same time, that they should get a jump on the weekend rush. All the machines were in use, number eight already rattling in a way I didn't like. Josie was smacking her lips over her empty mug and getting ready to start rummaging through her purse for the cigarette I wouldn't let her smoke. Outside, a man in a brown robe paced the sidewalk, sniffing out new turf. I had noticed him yesterday, a few stores down, and hadn't liked his fawning tone, the way he ma'amed me every second word when he asked for a handout. He reminded me of a cringing dog that would slink away if you looked him in the eye, then run up from behind to bite your ankle. He had to be watched.

It wasn't that I didn't think about Gina. I did. I felt her absence as a vague dread all day, a heaviness I could hardly carry around, but what could I do? People still had to wash their clothes, Josie still needed a warm, dry place to sit, and the brown-robed man outside had to be watched. Should I have simply told them all that I was very sorry, but my defining moment had arrived, and I had to leave them to pursue it? Possibly. A hero would have—or, like Lord Jim, would have hidden out in shame the rest of his life for failing to. But I was always more partial to Penelope than Ulysses, and have long thought that Lord Jim should have gotten over it, on with it, lived his life instead of mourning the one he wished he'd had. It was eleven o'clock on a busy Friday morning. I had a job to do, things to keep going, people besides Gina counting on me. I waited until Marlene relieved me at five.

Polly's was closed when I got there. A young woman—the same one I'd spoken to earlier, I assumed—was locking the door.

"We're closed," she called through the door, shaking her head at the same time and crossing her hands back and forth over each other in case I somehow hadn't gotten the point.

"Is Polly still here?" I asked through the glass.

"We're closed," she motioned again.

"I know," I shouted. "But I need to see Polly. I spoke to you earlier. I'm Gina's friend."

Those must have been magic words because a moment later I was inside, inhaling the sweet smells of puppy fur and cedar cat litter, standing face to face with a friendly-looking middle-aged woman who in no way resembled the pet-pimp Gina's descriptions had created in my mind. She introduced herself as Polly and said she'd been hoping I would call back or stop in, that she too was wondering about Gina.

"It's not like her to just not show up like this," she said. "I mean, we've had our moments—I don't think this was her favourite job in the world—but she was never irresponsible." Polly thought about that to make sure it was true, then said again, "She's not an irresponsible person. If she was going to be so much as ten minutes late, she phoned."

I wondered about the missing fifty dollars, how that fitted into Polly's notions of responsibility, or if petty thievery was in a different category from being where you said you would be, and phoning if you wouldn't.

"Did she ever take money from you?" I heard myself blurt out. Polly looked me over, appraising, and took her time in answering. "Is that what this is about?" she asked, suspicion beginning to change her face. "She take off with some money of yours?" "No, no," I assured her quickly. Too quickly, I could see. Her face was quickly closing in on itself. There was almost no trace of the friendly concern she'd greeted me with. "I'm a friend of hers. Really. I'm not trying to track her down for money, or anything." Too much protesting. It sounded overdone even to me. "I'm just trying to figure out what might be going on with her, and she told me that you thought she'd taken some money from you."

Polly nodded, still appraising, reappraising. I suspected she never stopped doing that no matter how long she knew someone, that she wasn't the type of woman who could be won over once and forever.

"Let's just say Gina and I had a difference of opinion about the till one night," she said. She was protecting Gina. I wondered why, who from, then realized. From me, of all people. The idea of it, the absurdity of it, made me feel oddly giddy. Just the thought that Gina might need protection from . . .

"She felt bad about it," I said, afraid I might start laughing in some strange unstoppable way. "Really bad," I added, gratified to see Polly's face soften minutely.

She shrugged. "It happens," she said. "There was just the one time with Gina. And there *were* a few big sales that day."

I glanced around the store wondering if there was some rare kind of hamster that sold for fifty dollars. I couldn't imagine it. They all looked the same to me, running endless, stupid circles around the wheels in their cages, peering through the bars with their noses twitching. I wondered if they really thought they were going somewhere, or if they were in it for the exercise, and how many revolutions it took for them to tire of it. Maybe they never tired of it. I could see one reason working here might have driven Gina crazy.

"To tell you the truth, I'm a little worried about her," Polly said. "I've had employees who thought they didn't have to show up or call in, but I can't see Gina pulling that kind of stunt."

I agreed it wasn't like Gina, and in the second it took to agree with Polly, the vague unease I'd been feeling all week sharpened into fear. I looked at her, unable to say anything for a few minutes. "What should we do?" I asked finally.

She shrugged. "I don't know."

I didn't either. The demands of the situation felt beyond my scope. It was a familiar feeling. I wondered if other people felt, on a regular basis, that they weren't brave enough, smart enough, enough in general, for the demands of their own lives.

"It's not like we're family or anything," Polly said. "Does she have family, or a boyfriend? Someone who would be in a better position to know whether or not this is something to panic over?"

"No," I said, and realized that, at that moment, the two of us were probably the most constant people in Gina's life, the only ones who saw or spoke to her every day, the first who would notice if she fell off the face of the earth. Or was pushed.

"Where is her family?"

"She doesn't really have one."

"What about friends?" Polly asked.

"Me," I said. "And some of the women where she used to work." Lois was the name that had come up most often. Teresa Marie, but she was gone.

Polly nodded slowly, putting it together. "Have you tried going over to her place?"

I had, had stood with my ear to her door just the night before, hoping to hear the rhythmic breathing that would assure me she was just sleeping something off.

"I think one of us should call the police," Polly said.

I nodded dumbly, relieved and ashamed that someone other than me had a plan of action.

"Do you want to?" she asked.

"I could," I said, then realized I couldn't. I couldn't bring myself to answer their questions, to supply them with information about her that would find its way into their files, their computers, their lunchroom conversations, but not do a thing to find her. If they hadn't managed to find any of the other missing women until some street person poked a decaying limb while scavenging through a dumpster, or some construction worker uncovered a head when he was trying to dig a foundation, why would they be able to find Gina while she was still alive, on the move, *trying* to elude everyone? Because she was alive. That much I knew. Had to believe.

"On second thought, why don't you go ahead and call them," I said.

Polly waited for me to explain my change of mind. When I didn't, she said, "OK." We stood around a while longer. I decided I didn't like her. For no good reason. For no reason at all. I didn't think I could spend one more second looking at her mild face.

"What are you going to do?" she asked.

"I don't know," I said. There seemed to be only two options: to wait or to look for her while I waited. "Look for her, I guess."

Polly nodded. "Let me know if you hear anything, will you?"

It was the way she asked *will you?*—unsure, like a supplicant who thought herself unworthy—that made me tell her I would.

5

Gina's grandfather died building the Golden Gate Bridge. It was one of the first things she ever told me, one of those pieces of information that are given to you early in a relationship, then forgotten, lost in the wake of everything that follows.

"You mean he fell off?" I asked.

"Or jumped. I've always had the feeling he jumped."

"Why?"

Gina shrugged.

"Was he depressed or something?"

She looked at me blankly. "Why would he be depressed?"

"*I* don't know. Why would he have jumped off a bridge?"

"Not *a* bridge. The Golden Gate Bridge." She smiled. "Maybe he liked the feeling of falling."

"People don't go around throwing themselves off of bridges for the thrill of the fall," I said.

"And how would you know?" she asked, her smile beginning to mock. "People will do almost anything for a good fall, you know."

"It was probably an accident," I said, sidestepping the challenge I saw in her smile and heard in her voice. I wondered if the story was even true. Probably her grandfather was still alive, trembling in some horrible nursing home, terrified of losing his footing. "Lots of people died building that bridge."

"I guess," Gina said, her smile fading, emptying her face.

I thought about that conversation as I walked along Hastings Street over to Xandu's. I don't know what made it come into my mind after all that time, but as I passed under a streetlight I saw Gina as she'd looked that night, her eyes shadowed by the light that hung too low over my kitchen table, her mouth twisted into the smile I'd interpreted as mocking. It could have been mocking, but could as easily have been questioning, nervous, self-mocking. The story could have been about her grandfather, herself, a confession, an invitation, a lie, a well-practiced piece of her repertoire that she performed for anyone she thought hungry enough to lap it up. I had lapped it up, incorporated into the core of my relationship with her the titillation I'd felt as she spoke, the anticipation of previously unimagined possibilities. I tried to remember how, exactly, the story of some working Joe plunging headlong to his death had aroused in me a sense of unimagined possibilities, but couldn't.

Xandu's flashing lights interrupted my thoughts. Still a block away, they caught my eyes and held them. Only the right nipple flashed—a round red bulb winking and beckoning over the sign promising "Live Girls." The left had burnt out, leaving the come-on unbalanced, oddly disturbing. It's just a light bulb, I told myself, but it felt like more. I had to fight with myself to press forward.

"You here to audition?" the bouncer at the front door greeted me.

"No," I said. He didn't step aside. "I'm here to see a friend," I added, as if I had to have a reason.

Nothing in his face moved. "Who's your friend?"

"Gina," I said, trying unsuccessfully to think of her stage name.

"Never heard of her."

I wanted to turn around, head home, maybe take in a movie along the way, a cup of tea at George's, but I made myself stare into the beefy face that blocked my entry.

"You got a rule that says no women customers?" I asked. My voice came out higher than I would have liked, with a bit of a quaver at the end, but his eyes shifted. Intelligent eyes, small as a pig's. I met them and didn't blink. He stepped aside without a word. I kicked myself later for thanking him.

"You here to audition?" the bouncer in the checkroom asked.

"No," I said, keeping my jacket.

"Too bad," he smiled.

I flushed, despite myself, at the thought of anyone wanting to see more of me than he already had.

"I'm Ron," he said.

"Hi Ron. Is Gina working tonight?" I asked.

He looked puzzled. "Gina?"

"Yeah. Tall, short dark hair . . . Kobra," I said, remembering.

"Yeah, yeah, I know her. But she hasn't worked here in months."

I was surprised by how much I'd been counting on finding her here, on everything returning to the kind of normal that, just a week before, I'd been so anxious to shatter.

"I thought maybe she . . ." I wasn't sure what I had thought.

"Mind if I . . . ?" I stopped myself from asking his permission to enter, but he granted it anyway. "Go ahead," he said, gesturing toward the main bar.

I had expected a tight press of bodies, a haze of smoke, the smell of fresh sweat, but the place was half empty and smelled mostly of cigarettes and Lysol. It was hard to believe that this was the room where Gina had spent so much of her time. She hated plastic and vinyl, thought fake wall panelling should be banned, as well as the colours orange and brown if people were going to insist on using them together. She had led me to believe that Xandu's was an old theatre, "a real heritage building," she'd said. I had imagined plush seats and velvet curtains, all in shades of magenta, crimson, burgundy, not this industrial lunchroom with the lights turned low.

I scanned the room, taking in groupings, avoiding the drunken noises coming from the far corner, trying to find a place to put myself. There was an empty table in the centre of the room. I sat down, then realized it wasn't right. Too close to the stage. I looked around, eyed another empty table near the back and started making my way toward it, self-consciously, clumsily, certain that every man in the place was staring at me, sizing me up. I was surprised, when I sat down, to realize no eyes had followed me. I had no idea what to do next.

On stage, Candy was finishing her routine. A boring routine to match her boring name, every move predictable and only half realized. Exactly the type of routine that Gina criticized. "They wonder why they don't get the tips I do," she'd told me more than once, "but most of them aren't willing to put the work in." I saw what she meant. Candy couldn't seem to take her clothes off and dance at the same time. "It's harder than it looks," Gina had told me, "but they don't even bother to practice. They all seem to think they're on their way to some place better."

I wasn't sure Candy did. She seemed tired, mostly. The men seemed tired too, bored, except the group in the far corner. They were irritated. "Come on baby," they called out, impatient. "Let's see some beaver," one finally shouted. Candy ignored them. She raised her hands over her head and turned a lopsided pirouette.

A waitress glided past me without stopping to ask if I would like anything. I tried to remember what I had thought I would accomplish by showing up at Xandu's. I turned the coaster over and something in the motion of my fingers reminded me of Josie. I pushed the coaster away, but then couldn't figure out what to do with my hands. I decided to leave, had made it halfway across the room when a male voice announced that Lois was taking the stage. I sat back down in time to see the waitress who'd ignored me glide onto the stage.

Lively and athletic, Lois' dancing spread a wave of energy through the room. She'd chosen "She's No Lady, She's My Wife" to open her set and she played it like slapstick. The far corner laughed as she rolled her eyes and danced around the stage, alternately sweeping with the broom she was holding, then humping it. The next song was slower, and as she started removing her clothes she directed more attention to the audience. She paid particular attention to the far corner, winning them over. Gina had told me that you had to convince every man in the room that you were dancing for him alone. Lois was doing a good job of it. When BB King started singing "The Thrill Is Gone," a voice called out "No way, babe. It's still there. You can feel it if you want." She smiled at him, and ran her fingers down the length of her broom. Other voices called out to her and she licked her lips or pinched her nipple for every one. As men waved bills at her, she lowered her hips to receive them in her G-string. She danced a four-song set, each song slower and bluesier than the one before. Her G-string was a chain of folded bills when she left the stage.

"Great act," I said as she breezed by my table a few minutes later.

It was obviously an opener she had heard before. Disdain soured her features before her professional smile reasserted itself. "Thanks," she said. Something about her posture made me think of a Brownie leader, though it could have been the general straightness of her. Everything about her was straight—her blonde hair, her white teeth, her tidy body. Nothing curled, curved or swelled out of line. Even her freckles were sprinkled along the bridge of a small straight nose. "Can I get you something?" she asked.

"Coke," I said, but as she went to get it, I followed her. "I'm sorry," I said, before we reached the bar. "I didn't really come in here for a drink. Or to watch the show."

She waited, her face giving nothing away.

"I'm a friend of Gina's," I said, expecting those four words to work as magically on Lois as they had on Polly.

"That's good," she said flatly.

I wondered if she thought I was a cop.

"My name's Tova."

"That's good," she said again. "So do you want your Coke or not?"

"No."

She moved away from me before I had a chance to ask her about Gina. I considered returning to my table, trying to catch her attention long enough to ask if she'd seen Gina, but I felt uneasy. She obviously wanted nothing to do with me—no one at Xandu's seemed to—and the place was filling up with customers. Real customers. I was the only woman in the place not on stage or working the floor. I sensed that if anyone started up with me I would be on my own. Worse, I worried that Lois might say something about me to someone, set me up in some way, ask the wrong person who I was and why I was nosing around about Gina. I went back to my table to get my jacket and made my way along the rear wall to the exit.

"Find what you were looking for?" Ron asked. I didn't like his tone or the way the lower half of his mouth hung open as if it could no longer contain the drool that was pooling under his tongue.

I ignored him but nodded at Pig Eyes as I approached the door, hoping it would make him move out of my way. It didn't. I had to brush against his belly as I pushed my way out the heavy door onto the street.

A thick fog had moved in, blurring and softening the edges of the street, consuming its lights. It soothed me—its moist embrace, its heaviness like a protective arm draped over the shoulder of the city. I realized it had been a mistake going into Xandu's like that— cold, unprepared—but that was all it was, a mistake. And it was only Friday night. I still had the entire weekend. Two full days and nights. I could start over again in the morning.

The phone rang at 6:00. Marlene, all apologies for waking me, asking if I could take her shift.

"Today?" I lifted one corner of the blind. Daylight was still over an hour away, but I could see from the halo around the streetlight that the fog hadn't begun to lift.

"I know it's last-minute, but I feel like shit."

Marlene was in the middle of a divorce. Her husband seemed to spend most of his time parked outside her apartment building, staring into her window. She often felt like shit.

"He was there all night. Every time I looked out."

She shouldn't have looked out, I thought, but didn't say. "Have you called the cops?" She had a restraining order and a lawyer, but it didn't seem to matter.

"They said they'd come by, but it's too late. He's gone now."

When I didn't say anything right away, she said, "You have to do my shift for me. I just can't go in today. I can't explain it. I just can't." With each *can't* she inched closer to hysteria.

"But if you let him make you a prisoner, then you're giving him exactly what he wants," I heard myself saying, like some parrot who'd been placed in front of the TV shows Marlene regularly quoted to me. I heard one of her kids wail in the background, then Marlene's voice, ashamed, "I know," as if what I said was true. As if there was something wrong with *her* for not shrugging him off and skipping cheerfully to the laundromat to put in her eight-hour shift. I wondered if there was some self-help book that offered tips on how to maintain a more positive, winning attitude while your husband sits outside your apartment waiting for an opportunity to blow your head off.

I told her I would take her shift. Ever Marlene, she didn't thank me, just said OK, as if it was the very least I could do.

Josie wasn't on the front stoop when I got to work. I knew she wouldn't be—she stayed away from Marlene's shifts—but I was oddly unsettled by her absence. I found myself waiting for her to appear out of the fog, missing the smell of her, the muttering vigil she kept over my shift. I wondered where she spent her weekends, if there was someone else's coffee she drank, someone else's workday she watched over.

My mood, as the drop-offs began to pile up, was vile, as if much more than one day had been stolen from me. I couldn't decide if I was angrier at Marlene—who had been less than sympathetic when Lynn and I split up—or her husband, who had not only ruined Marlene's day, but now had ruined mine as well, not to mention all of their kids'. Five days stolen, all by one prick. And that was just today. It was amazing, really, that no one seemed able to stop him. I could just imagine if he'd spent the night sitting in front of some businessman's house. Some judge's house. Someone he wasn't married to. *Call the cops*, I'd suggested, as if that would do anything. I tried to think of something that might. A trap, maybe. A live trap. One of those leg-hold things. Let *him* spend his days trying to gnaw off living parts of himself. The thought of that cheered me slightly, though, of course, it was possible that that was exactly what he was doing—that he'd mistaken Marlene for a live trap, that she was a live trap for him. I was still pondering that when Lois came up to the counter.

"I hoped I'd find you here," she said.

The switch in her tone and demeanour toward me was so complete I didn't know how to respond.

"Gina told me you worked here," she said.

"I'm usually off on Saturdays."

"Then we were meant to connect today," she said, grinning in a way I couldn't interpret. In daylight, she seemed younger than she had at the bar. With her pressed jeans and stiff cotton shirt, she looked like a prep school girl who hadn't noticed that her circumstances had changed. I looked at her feet, half expecting to see penny loafers. She was wearing running shoes, damp from the drizzle.

"I'm sorry about last night," she said. "I couldn't talk."

"You could have just said that."

"I just did."

"I mean last night."

"I've already apologized. Which is more than I can say for you."

"Me?"

"For your incredible stupidity."

"For my incredible stupidity," I repeated. Stupidly.

"And you can drop the wounded martyr bit," she said.

I stared at her, trying to see what Gina could have possibly seen in her.

"You come into a bar where you know absolutely nothing, zero, except that some pretty nasty stuff has been going down. You make no attempt to blend, like maybe finding some guy to come in with. No. You come in alone, stand out like some kind of mutating wart, start asking questions, not caring in the least who you might be putting into a tight spot. And then you have the nerve to act like some martyr with sensitive feelings because I call you stupid."

All said in the quiet, even conversational tone most people would use to give directions or describe their job to someone they knew wasn't interested.

"So I take it you also don't buy Gina's story," she said, as if she hadn't just called me a wart, stupid, worse than useless.

"What story?" I managed to ask.

She looked at me closely. "Why did you come in asking for Gina?"

I looked at her just as closely. "I didn't know it was a crime to look for a friend at her former place of work."

"I didn't say it was a crime. I said it was stupid, and you have to admit that it was." She didn't smile, but some feeling I couldn't read softened her features.

"What story of Gina's?" I asked.

"Didn't she tell you she was going to Tofino for a few days?"

"No," I said, relief, hurt and embarrassment flooding me all at once. "She didn't tell me anything." I could hear the hurt creeping into my voice in the form of a slight whine and hoped Lois wouldn't call me a martyr again.

Lois thought for a moment. "Yeah. Well, maybe you're someone she doesn't like to lie to." I noted the present tense and searched her mouth, her eyes, the set of her jaw for clues, but couldn't find any. She had the stillest face I'd ever seen.

"What are you staring at?" she asked.

"Sorry," I said, looking away.

"No, really. Do I have poppy seeds or something stuck between my teeth?"

"No," I said, relieved to see a smile I could interpret. "I'm just trying to place you."

"Right here, in front of you," she said, then, without so much as a pause, "I'm from Idaho, originally. Pocatello. Did you pick up my accent or something?"

"Yeah," I lied. "I don't think I've heard a Pocatello accent before."

"Then you can count yourself lucky," she said, really opening up her smile now. Such a tidy smile. I thought of Gina's elastic face, the emotions—usually conflicting—that played across it, and asked what, exactly, Gina had said to her.

"Just that she'd had it with Polly's, and was going to Long Beach for a few days to think things over."

"Alone?"

"Supposedly."

"In the middle of November?"

Lois shrugged. "I don't buy it either."

"Why not?" I asked.

"For one thing, Gina hates the ocean."

I tried to think if I knew that.

"A customer offered to take her to the Oregon coast once. The way she looked at him, you would have thought he'd suggested a weekend in Hell."

"Maybe it was the company," I said. Or maybe she didn't like Oregon, for some other reason. Maybe her period started right at that moment. Maybe she just didn't like the way he smelled.

"Gina's not in Tofino," Lois said.

"Where do you think she is, then?"

"Well now, that's the point, isn't it?" She leaned closer to me, both elbows on my counter. I realized we'd arrived at her purpose in coming in. "Seems to me, if Gina wanted us knowing where she was, she would have told us, don't you think?"

"Not if something happened to her," I said, ignoring the line of customers growing behind Lois.

"Like what? If something had happened to her she wouldn't exactly have been given advance warning. People don't go around making up lies to tell their friends before something happens to them, unless they're in control of it."

She had a point, though I wondered why Gina hadn't bothered to lie to me.

"She probably wants to be left alone," Lois added.

"But why?"

"I don't know *why*," Lois said, her voice beginning to tighten. In irritation, I thought.

"Is something going on at the bar?" I asked.

"Like what?"

"*I* don't know."

"You're damned right you don't," she said, her voice so tight I could barely hear it above the rumble of the dryers. "I can't tell you what to do," she said. "But if you're half as worried about Gina as you claim to be, then try laying off her for a while."

I wondered where she got off telling me what to do with Gina, what business it was of hers.

"Gina's my friend," I said. "I'm worried about her."

"Yeah, well, you're not helping any coming into the bar like that asking after her."

I felt a flush spread across my face as I realized she might be right. I asked if she could meet me later for coffee.

"What for?"

"Because I can't talk now." I gestured to the line of customers growing behind her.

"I work later," she said.

I suggested another time when she wouldn't be working.

"Stay away from the bar," she said in a soft, even voice, then she stepped away from the counter, out the door.

Scared, I thought, even before I started apologizing to my first waiting customer. Lois probably got stiller and softer the more terrified she was. Marlene shriller and more obnoxious. And Gina simply disappeared. I was surrounded by scared women, and I, of the narrow ruts and small gestures, had only just noticed.

How long had Gina been scared, I wondered, and of what? Of being Vancouver's next sacrificial offering, the next disposable woman offered up to whatever it was in some men that refused to be appeased? Or was it a more usual horror: her own life catching up to her, demanding a face-to-face meeting.

I thought again of the story she'd told me about her grand-father. Had she been trying to tell me something about herself? That she would jump, rather than fall, if it ever came down to that? I'd listened, titillated, hearing only a half-mocking invitation to leave my crabbed little life behind and dive eternally into the thrill of the fall. No wonder she called me a voyeur. It was hard not to be one with her, but maybe she'd hoped I would try a little harder than most.

6

I spent a bad afternoon. Everywhere I looked I saw evidence of a neglected life, my life, falling in around me. The laundromat was clean enough, but shabby, and the colour I'd chosen was wrong—I could see that now. *Sand*, the painter had called it, promising it would pick up and reflect all the warmer hues of the room, but in the absence of warmth, it had retreated to the colour of congealed oatmeal. Greyish-beige, lustreless, without hope—this is what I had chosen, what I offered to others. And underneath the dull paint, what looked like mushrooms beginning to sprout on the patch of wall by the radiator that I'd been meaning to replace since last November's flood. I looked closer. They were mushrooms. Small mushrooms, to be sure, almost shy—as if they'd realized, too late, that this was no rain forest—but definitely mushrooms. I brushed off their caps then turned my gaze inward.

The scene worsened. My life seemed a litany of almosts, not quites, next times, if onlys. I was a careful person, always choosing to work with a net—a steady job, well-worn rituals and conventions that gave form to my days and relationships—but somewhere along the way, I'd started operating so close to the net that I had become entangled in it. I'd wrapped it around me like a cocoon, emerging occasionally, a moth drawn to any flame burning around me, flitting uselessly around other people's light.

Something shifted in the room, drew my gaze back out. The fog had cleared. Pale sunlight leaked through the front window. The first sunlight in weeks; I wasn't ready for it. I felt exposed, craved the cover of darkness, the comforting fog. I squinted against it and saw Marlene crawling in, also squinting.

"You look the way I feel," she greeted me. "No offence."

"Thanks," I answered.

"Is something the matter?" she asked, then without waiting for my answer: "I got here as soon as I could."

"How are you?" I asked, though the answer was obvious. Her face was puffy, her eyes dull. Her yellow hair was growing out, showing a quarter-inch of mouse at the roots.

She shrugged. She'd already told me how she was. I had spent my day off working because of how she was. It occurred to me that she probably found me as obtuse as I found her. "Busy day?" she asked, then, again without waiting for my answer, "Couldn't have been as bad as mine. The kids get so bent out of shape when they see me upset like this. Not that *he* could give a damn.

"I'm not the least bit interested in Jerry, believe me," she went on. I tried to remember who Jerry was. "But try telling Gabe that. I'm telling you, if I was interested in even half the guys he accuses me of screwing around with—I swear he must think I'm some kind of nymphomaniac."

I realized, as I half listened to the latest list of Gabe's accusations, that I was feeling odd, as if a weight was shifting somewhere inside me and I was reeling within myself. I had never admitted before what an utter failure I was. I'd always hedged, tried to look on the bright side, but now there didn't seem to be a brighter side. I was a failure. I hadn't had extraordinary expectations of myself, but I had assumed that whatever I did, I would do thoroughly. I had expected to love and be loved, to be a good friend, to take my life as far as it would go, even if in others' eyes that didn't seem very far—but I hadn't.

"Last week he went so far as to accuse me of sleeping with the best man at our wedding," Marlene was saying.

"You're kidding," I said as the murky depression of the past—what? months? years?—began to crystallize.

"No, I'm not kidding. God, you don't know how much I wish I were."

"What an asshole," I said, then realized that what I had thought was a sinking feeling seemed now to be just the opposite. I felt myself rising. Perversely buoyant. *A failure.* It was bracing to admit it.

"That's putting it mildly," Marlene said. Then, looking at me more closely, she asked, "Are you OK?"

"Yeah, why?"

"I don't know. You seem distracted. I don't know . . . strange. No offence."

"I'm not strange," I replied. "I'm just your basic generic failure."

"Don't say that about yourself," Marlene said immediately, automatically, her eyes widening and flickering with the first signs of life since she'd crawled through the door.

"Why not?" I asked, my mood still soaring.

"Because it's not true."

"And how would *you* know?" I didn't want to bicker with Marlene, but it was annoying to be contradicted just at the moment I felt I might be approaching personal liberation.

"Nobody's a failure," she said, emphatically. "Sometimes we fail at things. We may *feel* like a failure then, but that's just low self-esteem. I mean . . ." she hesitated, then moved closer, and put her hand over mine. It was the first time we had touched since she found out I was queer. "You shouldn't feel like a failure, Tova. You're a beautiful person."

It didn't matter that I knew she stood in front of the mirror every morning and said those same words to herself—affirmations, she called them. I couldn't remember the last time anyone had touched my hand and used the word beautiful at the same time. I hadn't realized how hungry I was for it. My mood dove from the unprecedented heights it had just scaled to a new low. I wasn't just a failure, I was also lonely. Pathetically lonely. Nothing bracing about that.

"Thanks, Marlene," I said, afraid now I might start to cry. I felt my top lip quiver. Marlene gave my hand a squeeze.

"What are you going to do tonight?" she asked.

"I don't know. Why?"

"I don't think you should be alone."

"I'm OK. Really," I said, then remembered that she wasn't. She was the one whose ex-husband swore that if he couldn't have her no one would. She was the one who sat up night after night too terrified to sleep. And here I was trembling, close to tears.

"What about you?" I asked.

She shrugged. "I'll be all right."

"But do you have anyone who can come over, spend the night?"

She shrugged again. "I'll be all right. I'm used to him." She smiled. Reassuring *me*.

I tried to think of something to say. "You can always call me," I said.

To my shock, her eyes lit up. "Do you mean that?"

"Yeah."

"Really?"

"Yeah, really." I wondered what was so hard to believe.

"That means a lot to me," she said. It didn't seem like it should.

"You'd be amazed how wide a berth people like to keep between themselves and . . ." She hesitated, looking for the word. "And problems like mine," she finished.

I hadn't realized.

It was getting dark by the time I handed the place over to Marlene, but the sky was still clear, the North Shore mountains black against it. My mood hadn't risen once she released my hand. I didn't think I could face an evening alone. I tried to reassure myself that by admitting the worst, I had nothing more to lose, that my life couldn't possibly get worse, but I wasn't fooled. I knew it could get worse. Things could always get worse.

I walked by Gina's apartment, half expecting her lights to be on, then doubled back past Polly's—also dark—then over to George's. "What's happening?" he asked me, but I could see that he was busy. "Not a whole lot," I said, and continued on my way. I considered going to a movie, taking a walk by the harbour, buying a winning lottery ticket and planning my retirement, but there was nothing I felt like doing except having a cup of coffee with Gina. Or, in her continuing absence, having a cup of coffee with Lois and talking about Gina. I knew Lois wasn't interested. She couldn't have made that any clearer. To push her now would be pointless, to show up at the bar, stupid, possibly dangerous. But my life already felt pointless and stupid. And, despite myself, I did possibly dangerous things all the time. I drank Vancouver's water. I walked down the street. Sometimes, if I had the use of a car, I drove. Everything was possibly dangerous. You don't get to be safe until you're dead.

I went into a 7-Eleven to buy some Ajax—the ring around my tub had developed a peculiarly green tinge over the course of the week. *Organic material*, the city informed us. *Runoff in the reservoir.*

Nothing whatsoever to do with logging in the watershed, and perfectly safe to drink. I paid for the Ajax, and asked the clerk for a glass of water. The water was cloudy, more yellow than brown. I drank it down without even waiting for the sediment to settle, then, emboldened, headed over to Xandu's.

If Pig Eyes recognized me he wasn't giving it away. "You here to audition?" he asked when I tried to brush past him.

"Yeah," I said and could have sworn he smiled. Just for a second, and it could have been gas, but his lips did twitch as he said, "Go ahead."

"Back for more?" Ron asked.

"Yeah," I said, sticking to what worked.

The main bar was packed. A Saturday night crowd, drinking, smoking, making the noises men seem required to make if they're looking at naked women in the presence of other men. Through the haze of smoke I saw the object of the hoots, a lone woman, gyrating in yellow light. It was unflattering light, the light of bare light bulbs—harsh and unfriendly; it exposed rather than enhanced. I wondered if that was intentional and hated Roger. Again. Anew.

"You here to see me?" A low smooth voice in my ear. Greasy, I would think later, but not at the time. I jumped, froze, understood in my deepest cells why deer do what they do when pinned by a car's headlights. "Harry told me you were looking to audition."

Right on me. In my ear.

I turned around to face him. He was ready for me. His eyes met mine. Warm brown eyes. Interested. In me.

"Harry?"

"Didn't you tell the guy at the door you wanted to audition?" He smiled slightly. Slightly amused. By me, by the whole situation. His eyes were still on mine, waiting.

"Are you Roger?"

He was still smiling, eyes beginning to wander. *Roger sees young tits, his eyes go tilt*, I remembered Gina saying. Mine were over thirty and hard to locate under my denim jacket. He looked at my face again. I wondered what he saw.

"Why don't you come to my office," he said. It was worded as a question but felt more compelling. It was his eyes. If I could just get out from under them. I glanced away.

"What for?" Out of the corner of my eye I saw Lois moving through the crowd. She was holding a full tray of drinks. She saw me then looked away. I wondered if she would pretend she didn't know me or come over. I didn't know what to hope for.

Roger hadn't answered. I looked at him again. I didn't like the expression on his face. Still interested, no longer amused. Whatever warmth I thought I had seen was gone.

"What do you want here?" he asked.

"I'm looking for a friend."

"Who's your friend?"

"Her name's Pamela," I said. I was hot in my jacket, getting hotter. I can just leave, I managed to think, but I couldn't. I felt rooted to his ugly floor, pinned by his beautiful eyes made ugly by what I saw in them.

He waited.

"I'm looking for Gina," I said.

He smiled. "That's better."

I realized we were playing a game, had been playing since he sidled up behind me. He was winning.

He was still smiling. Warm again. Maybe he'd been warm all along. I was unbearably hot, but afraid if I took off my jacket I'd have huge sweat bands under both arms. I wiped the sweat off my nose.

"Can I get you a drink?"

"Thank you," I said. I meant for offering. I hadn't meant I accepted, but he was already snapping his fingers. Lois delivered the orders she was carrying then came over to take ours.

"How you doing?" she said to me. I wondered if she was acknowledging that she knew me or if that's what she said to every customer.

"Fine," I answered.

"What'll it be?" Roger asked me.

"Coke," I said.

Roger made a face. "Come on. I'm buying. Rum and coke," he said to Lois.

"Light on the rum," I added. I wasn't sure if Lois heard me.

"Coffee for me," Roger said. I hated him.

"Now what's this about Gina?" he asked as soon as Lois left to fill our orders.

"Nothing really. I just haven't seen her for days and I wondered if she might be here."

Roger thought about that. "She hasn't worked here for months," he said.

"Yeah, I know that, but she wanted her old job back. I just thought maybe . . ." I didn't mention that the day she disappeared she had said something about talking to Roger, about how she had gotten the feeling he might give her back her job. I wondered now what else they might have talked about.

Roger smiled. "I like Gina. She's a good person. A sweet person. She a close friend of yours?"

"Pretty close." I didn't care that he was pumping me, that I was missing an opportunity to pump him, possibly glean crucial information. I just wanted to get through the conversation and out onto the relative safety of the street.

"I'm sorry it didn't work out for her here, but . . ." He flashed a toothier variation of his smile. "This is a business I'm running. A girl lets herself go, I have no choice. I have to let her go. No matter how much I like her. And I like Gina a lot. She's a really sweet girl."

Lois returned with our drinks. Roger's coffee already had cream in it. I realized with horror that my drink had probably been poisoned. That this is where we'd been heading, where he'd been leading me. He was planning to knock me out so he could drag me to his office and kill me.

"Cheers," Roger said, lifting his cup at me.

"Cheers," I said, and took a tiny sip. It was straight Coke. Not a drop of rum. I silently thanked Lois' departing back, and swore I would make it up to her, somehow, even if that only meant never showing up at Xandu's, never bothering her again. I took another, longer swallow, enjoying the coolness of the liquid sliding down my throat. I resisted the urge to pick up the ice cubes, rub them over my face, then drop them down my shirt.

"Nice place you got here," I said, looking around. I was trained to take responsibility for conversation on a date with a man and this was as close to a date as anything I'd experienced in ten years.

"Thanks," he said. "I try to keep it comfortable. Clean, you know?"

I nodded.

"Naah," he said, smiling. "I don't think you do know. Gina ever tell you about the other places she worked? Before here?"

"No," I said, although she had mentioned working a circuit for a few years. A few nights in one city, then on to another. Hotel bars usually. Always having to be on, scoping out the new situation, figuring out who to suck up to, who to avoid, then having to move on as soon as she had it figured out.

"Gina was in pretty rough shape when she turned up on my

doorstep. Believe me," he added, as if I wouldn't. "I don't usually take on girls in that kind of shape, you know? I mean, this is a business, not some kind of treatment centre. But there was something about Gina, you know what I mean?" He looked at me. "Yeah, I can see that you do." He took a long swallow of coffee. "So I took her on."

"She liked working here," I contributed. My voice sounded chirpy. False. He didn't seem to notice.

"Yeah, I know she did. Most of the girls do. And if they don't, they're free to leave." I had heard Gina say that countless times. I hadn't realized they were Roger's words cloned to her tongue. "It's because I run a clean place. Most of the other places . . . well, you probably know, but here you either keep your G-string on, or you keep your six inches." He glanced at me and grinned. "I can see you know what six inches is. That's the rule. Six inches between a girl and a customer if she's not wearing a G-string. You don't like it, you find some place else to work. Same goes for the customer. I see a customer groping a girl who's flashing, he's out."

I sucked up the last bit of liquid from my glass, making more noise than I intended. "You want another one?" Roger asked.

"Oh no, that's OK," but he'd already snapped for Lois.

"And none of my girls are hookers. Some places, the dancing's just a front, you know?"

I nodded, unbearably thirsty.

"But here, every girl you see on stage is getting paid for what you see. What she does on her own time, that's her business, but when she's here, she dances, she serves drinks, she makes the customers comfortable. That's it. If I wanted to be a pimp . . . Believe me, what I'm trying to do here is harder than pimping. A lot harder."

I wondered if it was possible Roger thought I was an undercover cop. Anything was possible, I supposed. I saw Lois returning with my drink and felt my mouth start to water. She winked at Roger when she handed it to me.

"So what about Gina?" he asked.

"Nothing really," I said, guzzling my Coke down. I sensed an opening, an exit. I sprinted toward it. "She probably just took off for a few days. I don't know why I thought she'd be here."

But Roger wasn't stupid. "Maybe you thought somebody here would know where she was, where she took off to." He was watching me closely now. It didn't matter. I couldn't sweat any more heavily, get any redder in the face. Even if he thought I was a cop, he would have to figure I was a rookie, heading straight for the parking beat.

"Maybe," I conceded.

"Well, I don't know anything." His smile flapped into a leer. "We're not as close as we used to be, you know?" I didn't and didn't want to. "But maybe one of the girls knows something. She wasn't tight with too many—she could be a bit stand-offish, know what I mean?"

I was tired of having to nod or shake my head every time he uttered a sentence, but nodded anyway.

"Although one of them might know something. You never know. Lois might. She and Gina were getting pretty tight toward the end there. Want me to ask around and get back to you?"

"No, no, that's OK." I regretted drinking my Coke, began to feel dizzy, short of breath.

"You OK?" he asked me. I felt my chest tighten, the top part of my head start floating away from the bottom.

Roger was saying something, his face unsmiling. I tried to listen. "Do you need water?" he was asking, snapping his fingers frantically. Needlessly. Lois was already there.

"Look how pale she is," to Lois. "And sweating. Christ. Are you

OK?" to me. "I don't want any ambulances roaring up here," to Lois. "It's Saturday night, for crissake," I wasn't sure to whom.

"Are you all right?" Lois asked. At the sound of her voice I realized I hadn't been poisoned.

"I'm just feeling a bit shaky," I said to Lois. "I'll be all right. I have asthma," I added.

"You OK now?" Roger asked, looming.

"Maybe she needs a bit of air," Lois suggested.

"I think fresh air," I said.

"Yeah. Take her outside," Roger said, Gina momentarily forgotten.

I let Lois lead me away from Roger.

"What the hell is going on?" she asked me when she got me past Pig Eyes.

"I don't even want to talk about it right now."

"Think you might want to talk about it tomorrow?"

I said I might and we agreed to meet the next day at a coffee bar she knew on Commercial Drive. It was only when I turned the corner of my street that I realized I'd accomplished what I set out to do. Tomorrow, I'd be talking about Gina with Lois.

Andre, the super of my building, was shampooing the front hall carpet when I got home. A skinny man with bad teeth and a dirty blond ponytail that hung down the middle of his back, he looked like he'd spent a life flitting from shadow to darkened doorway, avoiding the direct light of sun or the gaze of passers-by. Gina declared him an addict the first time she saw him, but I felt there was something else wasting him, something deadlier than drugs pocking his cheeks and furring his teeth. "Like what?" Gina asked, nostrils flaring—she hated to be contradicted in any of her areas of expertise. "Disappointment," I ventured, to which Gina snorted.

"Try junk," she said. "Disappointed men wear short sleeves from time to time." I wished Gina could see him now, sleeves rolled up, revealing forearms as smooth as the underbelly of a fish.

"What's up, Andre?" I greeted him.

"Not much," he admitted. I liked that about him. He never pretended to have a million schemes up his sleeve. It was enough that he was trying to lift the smell of cat piss from a carpet.

"Any more complaints about me?" I rolled my eyes to the floor above us, apartment 2-C specifically.

"Aw, she's all right," Andre said. He refused to give in, wouldn't call her crazy, share a shrug and a smile of relief that there was at least one line we'd managed to stay on the safe side of. "Anyway, she's off you for now. She thinks it's the pigeons."

"What's the pigeons?"

"The noises she's been hearing. She thinks they're building a nest."

"A nest. Where?"

Andre smiled. "In your apartment."

I nodded, beginning to catch on. "And?"

Andre was still smiling, obviously enjoying this more than scrubbing cat piss. "And so she thinks I should poison them."

I started at the word poison.

"She wants you to poison an imaginary nest of pigeons?"

Andre nodded.

"And where, exactly, are you supposed to put the poison?"

Broad smile now, revealing both rows of fuzzy teeth. "In the nest."

"In the nest," I repeated, then understood. "You mean in my apartment."

The coincidence was unnerving. I was surprised at just how unnerving. I felt myself getting hot again, my chest tightening, my mind fluttering to the possibility that 2-C was no ordinary crank.

"Aw, Tova. Don't take it so seriously. Always so serious."

"It *is* serious. What if she decides in the middle of the night that poison's too slow, and hacking off the pigeons' heads is the way to go?"

"Just don't wear a feathered nightcap," Andre said, cracking himself up.

I generally trusted Andre's ability to tell the odd from the dangerous—that was one of the selling points of the building, that and the old-fashioned tubs and the view of the harbour with the mountains rising steeply out of it—but no one was infallible.

I tried to be extra quiet letting myself into my apartment, but the phone was ringing and I had to run across the living room to answer it. As I did, I could hear 2-C banging on my floor—her ceiling—with whatever it was she'd rigged up to communicate her displeasure with me. Her lethal hatred of me. I reached the phone in time to hear it click dead in my ear.

"Hello?" I said anyway, too late.

2-C was still banging. "Shut up," I called and, miraculously, she stopped. I went to run my bath and over the rush of running water I heard the pounding starting again, fainter, further away—she'd obviously changed rooms or instruments.

For the second time that day I decided I couldn't go on this way. I had never been a noisy person, but there was a limit to how quietly I could exist. Somehow, over the course of this day, I felt I had reached it. I wanted to be able to walk across my own apartment without someone pounding her protest, to run a bath, to boil water even if my kettle did whistle. It would even be nice to play music every so often. Rickie Lee Jones, Bonnie Raitt. I had read in more than one magazine that they'd both gotten their lives together over the period of time mine had fallen apart. I had always liked their music. Maybe their new albums would inspire me as well. I resolved to talk to Andre, but as I turned off the bath, I realized the banging wasn't coming from downstairs, and it wasn't the usual banging. Someone was knocking at my door. Andre. With a package.

"This came for you," he said, holding out a small brown box with my name and address scrawled across the front in Gina's large hand.

"When?" It was almost weightless.

"Yesterday. I meant to bring it by last night."

She'd arranged the stamps—all portraits of the Queen—like the petals of an aster around an empty centre. The postmark was smudged but legible. Vancouver.

"I meant to bring it by last night," Andre said again. "But . . ." He flashed a dingy smile.

"Yeah, I know. It's OK," I said automatically, though it wasn't. Had I known over the last twenty-four hours that she'd sent word, more than word, a package, complete with a flower-like arrangement of the Queen's disembodied head . . . then what? I wasn't sure, but it wasn't OK at all that Andre had held onto it.

"A secret admirer?" he asked, misreading my agitation.

"One of many," I said, and, radically impolite, started closing the door before he was ready to leave.

I tore open the wrapping. Inside, Gina had crammed the box full of paper, tissue paper, pink and crumpled as a crinoline. Balanced on top, like a wayward tiara, was her choker. She had cleaned it, buffed the chrome, at least. I could see her on Roger's shabby stage, her chrome shiny as the fenders of a new car.

The choker itself was soft, well worn and, contrary to what Gina had said, smelled of nothing but old leather. I poked through the tissue looking for a note and found a small piece of paper torn unevenly from a larger piece. *Sorry, love Gina,* was all it said.

And my phone was ringing again. Marlene. "I just got home and he's out there."

Her voice stopped me short. There was a vividness to it, an immediacy to her terror that cut through all the vague fears, anxieties and what ifs I'd been experiencing all day and evening.

"Where?"

"Same place as always. No matter which window I look out of I can see him."

I had seen the outside of Marlene's apartment. Four windows on the third floor of a boxy low-rise. He'd be sitting in his car, watching those four windows, waiting for her head to appear. And in the jerky movement that betrayed her fear as she pulled her head back out of his sight, his moment.

"Have you called the police?"

She hesitated.

"You have to call them, Marlene. He thinks he can keep doing this to you night after night, but he can't." Although I knew he could. "You can't let him keep doing this to you."

"I can't call the cops."

"Why not?"

"I just can't."

"They're not always useless," I said, misunderstanding.

"I don't want to make him mad." She said it so quietly I wasn't sure I had heard her right.

"He's trying to psyche you out," I said. "He's testing you to see if you'll get the restraining order enforced." How did I know? I'd never even met him. Most of them moved along when the police told them to, but every so often one of them blew. And took her along with him. Who was I to tell her what to do? I wasn't like

Andre. I couldn't instinctively discern odd from dangerous, bluff from threat. It was always a handicap—like having faulty pain sensors—but in this situation it felt potentially life-threatening. "Why don't you stop looking out the window?"

"I want to keep an eye on him."

"That's his whole point. He wants to make sure you're so busy keeping an eye on him that you never get your life back." What did I know about his goals, let alone what was required to take your life back?

She didn't say anything. I wondered what to say next. I felt I should be injecting a cool head into the situation, but instead was catching her fear. I realized I was clutching the phone. It felt warm and greasy against my ear.

"I'm calling the police," I said.

"He'll kill me."

"He won't kill you." Maybe he would. They say barking dogs don't bite, but some do, and in the absence of an intuitive knack for telling one from the other, you have to either avoid all dogs or risk getting bitten. "This can't go on."

Marlene didn't say anything.

"I'm calling the police," I said again.

"Call me right back," she whispered.

My fingers were shaking as I pressed 911. The voice at the other end was calming, the cool head I'd hoped to be. She repeated back all the information I gave her, reassured me someone would be there shortly, then asked for my name, number and address as well as Marlene's. When I called Marlene back her line was busy.

I repacked the pink tissue in the box Gina had sent me, placed the choker on my night table, the note in my drawer. Then I lay down and waited for Marlene's line to clear. My eyes were heavy, but my exhaustion wasn't as numbing as usual. Mostly I was lonely. Unspectacularly, achingly lonely. An unpleasant feeling, without the dazzle of grief or the sear of betrayal I'd felt the first months after Lynn left. It lacked even the challenge of the horror I'd felt earlier in the day when confronting the utter failure of my life. Dull, thudding loneliness. Far from the cutting edge of emotional experience. Commonplace. I wondered when it had taken me over, replaced the more acute feelings that had tied me to Lynn for so long, when the sharp longing for her had diffused into this impersonal ache. I closed my eyes, and when I opened them again, it was 4:00 A.M. By now Marlene was either dead or asleep. Same with Gina. I turned over, went back to sleep and woke up at 7:00. I reached for the phone and dialled Marlene's number.

"They arrested him," she announced, neither relieved nor triumphant. Mostly weary.

"And what happens now?"

"Now I get the kids off to my mother's so I can get in to work before you decide to fire me."

"I'm not going to fire you." It was strange to realize I had that power over her, her life. "What happens to Gabe now?"

"I have no idea. I guess they're going to hold him." She could barely drag the words out of her throat. In the background I heard two of her kids, possibly all three, arguing over something. "If you don't shut up I'm going to flush the stupid prize down the toilet," she yelled. The argument continued undiminished. "What are they thinking, putting one cheesy prize in a box of cereal? I mean, do they expect a bunch of kids to split it evenly down the middle? I mean, has one of those douche-bag executives ever actually sat down at a breakfast table with a bunch of kids?"

I assumed they had, but I was tired, hadn't slept well. I didn't feel like getting into an in-depth discussion about the expectations and life experiences of cereal company executives.

"Thanks for last night," she whispered, and I realized she was ashamed as well as weary.

"It's OK," I said. There was a moment of silence between us, comfortable, almost familiar, before we reverted to bidding each other "Have a good day."

7

Lois was waiting for me. She leaned against the doorpost of the coffee bar, hands in her pockets, her shoulders hunched against the day. "This all right?" she greeted me. She looked considerably less crisp than she had just twelve hours earlier. I wondered if she'd been to bed yet.

From inside the café I could hear men shouting, groaning.

"Soccer." She shrugged. "It's just ending."

Badly, it seemed. Another groan, then groups of men pooling on the sidewalk around us, yelling at each other in Italian.

A wall of smoke hit us as we walked in. Lois went to get our coffee while I claimed a table and cleaned off the sugar, ashes, and rings of coffee. The decor was similar to Xandu's—dim lighting, dark panelling, sticky undersurfaces. Obviously designed for men. I wondered if that was why Lois liked it. I didn't. The dimness, mostly. I was tired of half-light, of a pale sun that lacked the strength or will to fight its way through a few dirty panes and a filter of smoke.

"You get home all right last night?" Lois asked, returning with two espressos.

"Uh huh," I said, sipping at mine. It needed sugar, milk.

"Gulp it," she said, throwing hers back in two quick swallows. I followed and snapped into a level of alertness I wouldn't have thought possible from a drug that was legal.

"So what was going on between you and Roger?" she asked, but she was looking at my neck.

"It's Gina's," I said, fingering the choker.

"I know that."

"She sent it to me."

I expected Lois to jump: when? how? what did she say? is she OK?

"What were you talking about with him?"

Roger, she meant. All she could think about. Probably the only reason she'd suggested this meeting in the first place.

I told her and waited for her to slip off, out the door, having gotten what she came for. She nodded, considering. After a while she asked what I knew about the choker I was wearing.

As she asked, I could feel it tightening around me.

"Just that it belonged to a woman who's missing."

"Who's dead, you mean."

"How do you know?" I asked, but Lois ignored me.

"Why would Gina send you . . . that?" Her lip curled, just for a second, revealing a bit more of her teeth than I'd seen up to that point.

"I'm not sure," I admitted. At first I'd thought it was to insult me. There was something about the packaging, the enigmatic note, the careful choice of pink tissue. It had felt like yet another variation on Gina's never-ending leather-and-lace routine. A game, when I'd been hoping for contact. A put-down, as well aimed as a slap in the face. And yet, as I put it on—just for a second, just to see what it looked like, felt like against my skin—I'd remembered Gina's face as she talked about Teresa Marie, and felt entrusted. "Maybe because she knew I would wear it."

"Whatever you get off on, I guess."

"I'm not getting off on it," I said, though I didn't know how to explain the odd comfort of its weight on my neck, the feeling I had that, despite all appearances, Gina was finally trusting me with something. "How are you so sure Terry's dead?" I asked.

"I just am." Her tongue flicked her upper lip, searching for something.

The thought of Gina walking around with a naked neck suddenly sickened me. I touched the choker lightly.

"Guess Gina decided she wouldn't be needing that anymore," Lois said watching me.

"Why are you mad at her?" I asked.

"Why aren't you?" she shot back.

A fair question. I sipped at my empty cup, put it down. "I'm worried about her."

"Yeah, well, maybe you should save your worry for someone who needs it." As she said it, the corners of her mouth pulled down, just a fraction of an inch, enough to reveal fine lines that could only deepen. "Gina's like a stray cat. She doesn't need worrying over."

I wondered how many times she'd rehearsed that line.

"You should have seen her when she first showed up at Xandu's."

"Did you?" I asked.

Here Lois coloured slightly, a faint wash of blood as she admitted, "No, but Roger told me."

"Ah, Roger."

Her colour deepened. "He's not that bad."

I wondered what was it about Roger that made all the women around him chant that line like a mantra.

"He keeps a lot of kids off the street."

That was a new one. Xandu's as a social service agency.

"A real Sir Galahad."

"Huh?" The curled lip again.

"What did Roger have to say about Gina?" I asked.

"Oh, just what a mess she was. Her hair was so matted he had to cut it off." She met my eye. "Dried puke."

"Puke washes right off," I pointed out. "Dried or fresh."

Lois thought about that, shrugged.

"What is it with you, you and Gina both, that you seem to think he's some kind of guardian angel?"

She looked at me with her blank expression. "He did take Gina in. Cleaned her up, gave her work. That's what he does, you know."

I didn't.

"And then, the minute she gets her strength back—whoosh." Lois sliced the air with her open hand, a movement more like a butcher with a side of beef than a stray cat slipping off into the night. "And it's not the first time either. That's what her whole life has been like. She messes up, finds someone to take her in, then as soon as it begins to look like she might get it together, might actually get a life . . ."

"Gina tell you all this?"

"Roger did." She had the good grace to blush again.

"What did Gina tell you?"

Nothing. I could see it from Lois' face.

"Did it ever occur to you that Roger might have something to do with Gina's disappearance?" I asked.

Lois looked at me, blush receding. "Don't waste your worry," she said.

"But it's just not true that she took off as soon as she started getting it together. It's Roger who fired her."

She didn't argue. She reached into her purse and pulled out a package of cigarettes. "Mind if I smoke?" she asked, and actually waited for me to say OK before lighting up. She inhaled her first lungful, smiled, and said, "This is why I had to leave Pocatello."

"Why?" I asked, feeling I had just lost whatever grip I'd had on the conversation.

"Mormons don't smoke. Or drink coffee. Or tea. Or alcohol."

I wondered why she wanted me to know that, if it was possible she'd so recently left home that she wasn't used to having conversations with people who couldn't place her. Or if she still heard her parents' rules every time she lit up. I wondered, for the first time, how old she was.

"So you left Pocatello for a cigarette and a cup of coffee," I said.

"Exactly." She smiled. And because of what she'd just told me, I could see that same face upturned in some unforgiving pew singing a hymn to Jesus. If that's who Mormons sang to. "What about you?" she asked.

"What about me?"

"Why did you leave wherever you're from?"

I hadn't been asked a question like that in a long time.

"How do you know I didn't start out here?"

"Just a guess." Then, as if as an after-thought, "Gina told me you're Jewish." I must have looked surprised because she added quickly, "She only told me that when she heard about all the weird religious things my family believes. I mean, she didn't say anything bad about Jewish people or anything."

It occurred to me that Lois might be under eighteen.

"So?" she prodded.

"I'm from Montreal."

"Montreal," she repeated. Her relaxed vowels made it sound like some place foreign. "So why'd you leave?"

"Oh jeez, it was so long ago." As if I couldn't remember, couldn't still feel Lynn's hand on my thigh as we hit the Trans-Canada heading west.

"I bet I know," she said, inhaling another lungful of forbidden smoke.

"What do you know?" I asked.

"You left home to kiss girls."

"Gina talks too much," I said.

"She didn't tell me, I swear. But I'm right, aren't I? I bet your mother couldn't have been too thrilled when she found out about you."

Unscared, unstill, her face might even have been that of a sixteen-year-old.

"My mother left home long before I ever did," I said.

"Oh," Lois said. "Why?"

"How old are you anyway?" I asked.

"How old do you think?" she countered with an immediate pout. It was obviously a question she got asked a lot. I couldn't believe that I hadn't even noticed the woman I was talking to was a teenager.

"I'm nineteen," she said when she realized I wasn't going to guess.

"You're sixteen." Even as I said it I hoped she would contradict me.

"I'll be nineteen next week."

She was eyeing me, tense, ready to be up, out of there, on the next bus out of town if my face so much as twitched the wrong way.

"I'm not going to turn you in, Lois." I didn't add that she could trust me, because I didn't know if she could. But it was true I wasn't going to turn her in.

"I won't really be nineteen until the summer."

"Which summer?" I asked, remembering to smile.

"This coming summer. I swear to God."

"Stop swearing and get me another cup of coffee. With some milk in it this time."

When she came back I asked her how old she was when she started working for Roger.

"Eighteen," she said, with a firm smile.

I said OK, willing to back off on that, then, on a whim, asked what she knew about Gem.

"Gem," she repeated, like she'd never heard the name before, like she had to reach back through all her vast years of experience to check if she'd ever come across that name. "Is that her stage name?"

"She's not a dancer. She's a social worker. She looks for missing street kids."

"Oh yeah? And what does she do with them when she finds them?"

It hadn't occurred to me to wonder that. "I don't really know," I admitted.

"Are you going to eat all the chocolate on top of your cappuccino?" she asked and, having established her approximate age, felt free to reach over and skim it off with her finger.

"If she really were a social worker," she said, sucking the chocolate and foamed milk off her finger, "she wouldn't be looking for someone like me."

"Why not?"

"For one thing, I'm way too old. It's the ten-to-fifteen-year-olds they're after. And then, only if they're whoring, on the street or doing drugs. I'm not doing any of that."

"What *are* you doing?"

"What are *you* doing?"

Another fair question. I didn't answer. She might be more slippery than I, but I could be stubborn.

"So what about this Gem?" she asked. Again, as if she'd never heard the name.

"Lois," I began. ". . . Is that your real name?"

"Real enough." I let it go.

"I know you know who Gem is."

She must have felt her colour rising again, because she took a long time swallowing her coffee and held her head back further than she needed.

"What do you know about her?" I asked.

She shrugged.

"Did you know Gina was looking for her before she took off?"

By the sudden stillness of her face I assumed I had either surprised or frightened her with the question.

"No." Underneath her stilled features, one lone muscle in her jaw began to twitch. "Why would I? Why would I know anything Gina was up to? I was only a close friend of hers."

Her mouth twitched down, hard, revealing disappointment I would have thought would take longer than eighteen years to settle in. It wouldn't take much, I realized—a few more years, one particularly bad night—to sap her face of all signs of hope. I sensed she hadn't laid in a deep enough store of some essential nutrient before she set off from Pocatello, hadn't taken in enough of what she would need to see her through. Her face, pulled down like that, made me think of the hydrangeas Andre had planted. After months of rain all winter and spring, they still couldn't get through a two-week dry spell in the summer without drooping. "Shallow rooters," Andre explained to me once, and I recognized Lois as another.

"Gina let you down, didn't she?"

She nodded. I wanted to reach over and lift the corners of her mouth.

"Me too," I admitted, "but I'm also worried about her."

She didn't tell me to save my worry this time.

"I don't think she left town the way she did because things were going too well for her and she just couldn't handle it."

Lois managed a weak smile.

"I think she was scared of something," I said.

"What?"

"That's what I'm not sure of. I thought you might have an idea."

"Why?" she asked. "Why would I know anything?"

"Because you're also scared," I tried. She didn't sneer. "Maybe of the same thing."

She lit another cigarette and smoked it slowly. I didn't get the feeling that it had been worth leaving Pocatello for.

"Girls leave jobs all the time in this line of work. Leave town." She spoke with a deliberate slowness. A strange slowness. I sensed the words weren't hers, but had been said to her. By Roger. "Look at me. This is already the second town I've worked. My second country, for that matter. Gina's splitting is no big deal."

"What about Teresa Marie's?"

She shrugged again. "That's not that unusual either. Girls go missing." She thought for a moment. "That's just the way it goes in this business." I could almost see Roger's thick mouth as she said it, feel his greasy eyes sliding over me. "It's like miners getting buried every so often. It's like . . ."

"An occupational hazard," I filled in.

"Yeah, that's right. Stripping isn't like being a secretary, you know. It's risky. And either you can take the risk or you can't. If you can't, you're in the wrong line of work."

"Roger tell you this?"

"I do have a brain of my own, you know." Her expression remained empty even if she couldn't control the blood flowing beneath.

"If Roger's trying to tell you that it's OK that girls are disappearing, that it's all in the line of work . . ."

"He never said that."

"Then what did he say?"

"Just that it's a risky business. That he can't screen all the men who come in, and there's bound to be some guy now and then who seems perfectly normal until he sees you on stage and gets it into his mind that you're his." She checked my face. "You have to admit, it is a risky line of work."

She said it with evident pride.

"How many strippers and prostitutes do you figure have gone missing in Vancouver over the last few years?" I asked.

"Lots," she said, again with a certain swagger.

"Yeah, well, I bet if anyone ever cared to count, they would find at least as many wives who have gone under," I countered, wondering if that was true. "You want to live dangerously, get on the next bus back to Pocatello, marry some guy from your church, have a couple of kids, then wait and see if he turns out to be one of the weirdos."

"You don't know what you're talking about," she said, looking as if I'd just struck her across the face.

"I do, actually," I said, thinking of Marlene. "But let's say you're right. Let's say you really are living dangerously, right on the edge, a twentieth-century pioneer . . . Why would you want to? I mean why would you come all the way from . . ." I tried to remember what state she'd said Pocatello was in. "Where is Pocatello anyway?"

"Idaho."

I nodded. "Famous potatoes."

She smiled, a little grimly.

"So why would you come all the way from Idaho just to do

something that you think could get you killed? I mean, what is so great—"

"I wasn't molested or anything," she interrupted.

"I didn't say you were."

"That's what everyone thinks the second they meet you. If you like dancing naked for men it's because your father felt you up or something. It's like, no one believes you just happen to want a more exciting life."

I didn't ask why this particular kind of excitement. Why not climb a mountain, fall in love, row to Alaska with one arm tied behind your back? I was remembering excitement, the strange places I'd thought it might be hiding.

She shrugged as if I had asked. "That's just the way I am. I think it's in my genes." She smiled suddenly. A real smile, almost impish. "My grandfather jumped off the Golden Gate Bridge."

My response was physical, mostly. Fatigue washed with nausea.

"That was Gina's grandfather," I said.

"What are you talking about?"

"It was Gina's grandfather who jumped off the Golden Gate Bridge. For the thrill of the fall. She told me."

"Gina told you that?" Her lip curled again. "Gina doesn't even have a grandfather. She doesn't even have a family."

"She has a family," I said. "She just hasn't seen them since she was a kid."

"Yeah? Then why's she trying to steal mine?" Then, to prove it was her grandfather, she started telling me the entire history of her family, starting with Great-Aunt Emma, the first in her family to make it across the country to the community growing up around Great Salt Lake. She needn't have bothered.

"I believe you," I interrupted her.

She stopped, but only to say how much Gina pissed her off,

what a user she'd turned out to be. "That's the only reason she hooks up with people. To use them." The lines down the sides of her mouth were back. They'd be permanently set before she turned twenty-five. "I can just imagine what she's using Gem for. If that's who she's with," she added quickly.

"Is it?" I asked, and when she didn't answer, I asked who told her.

She looked at me as if I was a slow child she no longer had the patience to help. "No one *told* me. It's a rumour. Everyone's saying it. Even you're saying it." As if I wasn't included in "everyone."

"But why?"

Lois spoke slowly, as if I might not be able to follow. "Some of the girls at work are wondering what Gem's trip is about wanting to rescue all the street kids."

"What the hell do they think her trip is?"

"Beats me." She was staring at the choker.

I thought for a minute, then asked, "How old was Terry?"

Lois shrugged.

Sixteen tops, Gina had said.

"Was she one of the kids Gem was helping?"

Lois picked up a cigarette, then put it down without bringing it to her mouth. "She knew her."

"And?"

"And nothing."

I waited.

Lois picked up her cigarette again and lit it this time. "Terry was a really special girl," she said. "If you knew her . . ." She paused.

"What was she like?"

Lois thought about that. "It's hard to explain. Just really sweet, you know? Roger didn't usually like to hire Native girls. He said they were . . . you know . . . dirty." She glanced at me, a blush beginning to spread into her cheeks and neck. "Terry, too. He said that about her too, you know, even after . . ." She paused again. "But if you knew what she was like. She'd do anything for you—it didn't matter what. She didn't even have to hardly know you. That's just what she was like."

"Generous," I said.

Lois looked at me, puzzled. "Yeah, sort of. She was just . . ." Her eyes filled with tears.

"It must have been awful for you when she disappeared." My words felt stiff, stupid, but Lois nodded, her tears spilling over now. She wiped them away and stabbed her cigarette into the ashtray. We sat a while in silence. I realized my fingers were playing at the choker.

"Do you think Gem . . . ?" I stopped and tried to figure out what, exactly, was the question nagging at my mind. I went back to the beginning of the conversation. Gem. The girls at Xandu's wondering what her trip was.

"She couldn't let it go," Lois said.

"Couldn't let what go?"

"Terry."

"What do you mean, she couldn't let it go?"

Lois shrugged, her face stiffening again into her still mask. "Gina neither," she added.

"What do you mean?" I asked again, but Lois just shrugged. "Can you?" I asked. "Let it go?"

Lois shrugged again. "It's different," she said, and before I could decide what to say or ask next, she slid from her chair and out the door.

8

I walked slowly along the streets just west of Commercial, climbed the caged footbridge that crossed the railroad, and stood for a few minutes staring through the mesh wire to the tracks below. The tracks ran the length of the entire city, but this was the only caged crossing. "It's because of the projects," Gina said once, pointing her chin at the housing projects on the other side. "They asked for a bridge, so this is what they got. Dual purpose," she added, weaving her fingers through the mesh enclosure and pulling on it.

We had stood where I was standing now, trying to figure out what, exactly, the railroad officials thought people in projects might do if their bridge weren't encaged. Spitting and rock throwing were all I could come up with until Gina pulled down her jeans, squatted, and peed through the mesh onto the tracks below. It was exactly the sort of gesture that Lynn would have called futile, but ever since, this bridge had felt my own, personalized.

I squatted down, jeans fastened. A freight train rumbled toward me, and I started counting cars. Three Saskatchewan grain cars with their crossed sheaves of wheat, four Burlington Northerns, four Canadian Pacifics. My mind drifted.

I supposed I should be angry with Gina. Lois obviously was. Anybody with an ounce of self-respect probably would be. She had lied to me, repeatedly, from the first moment we met, and then split without so much as a nod in my direction. A person with a life would have told her to shove it long before now. Instead, I intended to look for her. Why, I wondered. Why Gina? Why now? She wasn't the first woman to go missing from my life, was a minor player compared to some. My mother, for one. Lynn. No doubt there was a psychological explanation, some complicated plot of misplaced drives, needs and affections. A person with a life would know it, know enough to let Gina go, swallow the urge to find her, find a good counsellor instead. But then, people with lives always seemed to be the ones who missed the spaces in between, the crawl spaces of what might have been and what might still be.

Andre was picking up used condoms and syringes from our front yard when I got there.

"What's the count?" I greeted him.

"Four condoms, one syringe."

Our numbers had been dropping. Between the Shame the Johns campaign over in Mount Pleasant and our own Neighbourhood Watch, the street trade was being pushed out of residential streets into the uninhabited industrial strips. Lethally dangerous for the prostitutes, but fewer condoms messing our yards.

"What's happening?" he asked, looking at me with his sad smile.

Maybe I'd been wrong about Andre. Maybe he wasn't disappointed at all. His sadness seemed too pure, uncut with the bitterness of rotting expectations.

"Not much." I tried to think of something to prolong the exchange. "Beautiful day."

He kissed his fingers, then released the kiss. To the day, I assumed.

"A friend of mine's missing," I said.

"That's not good," he answered, pursing his lips, returning his attention to the clean-up.

Idiot, I thought, meaning Andre. Or maybe he wasn't. Maybe his good instincts extended to knowing what required his attention and what wasted it.

"Since Wednesday night. Maybe afternoon. This is hers." I touched the choker. "Was. That's what was in the package that came for me the other day. She sent it. "

Andre looked up. "Before or after she went missing?"

"After."

He nodded, pursed his lips again and turned back to his yard.

"She just took off. Didn't tell anybody." Didn't tell me, anyway.

Andre began piling pine needles around the roots of one of the rhododendrons that lined the front walk. "Acid-loving," he said, patting the pile. "Rhodos just love their acid."

"I talked to another friend of hers today, a girl she worked with. She said she wasn't worried, but I think she is. She seemed . . ." I tried to think of what it was, exactly, that Lois had seemed. I couldn't hold a clear picture of her in my mind.

Andre didn't seem impatient for Lois to come into focus. He was lightly scratching the earth near the surface roots with his fingers. I watched for a while, still not quite ready to face my empty apartment, the rest of my day, then asked him where he was from.

He looked up, as surprised by my question as I was.

"You mean where I started out?"

"Yeah."

"Portugal. Sunny Portugal."

I tried to imagine him some place perpetually sunny, but couldn't. Couldn't imagine him any place other than our grey stucco low-rise.

"So what brought you to Vancouver?"

"A ship." He chuckled softly and began to sing a song in a language I assumed was Portuguese. "You know that song?"

I shook my head.

"Then you've never loved a seaman."

I had to smile. "There's lots I haven't done."

He laughed out loud. I had heard him laugh before, but always from another room, from down the hall. Until now all I'd ever elicited was his dingy smile.

"So you were a seaman?"

He laughed again. "Thought I'd be. I left home at fifteen, told my Mama I had things to do. I got myself a job on a freighter. Shit work, you know?"

I knew.

"Hauling ropes and crates. But who cared, right? Hard work, salt air, a pretty girl in every port. The sailor's life was the one for me. You know that one?"

I nodded.

"Only one problem."

His eyes lit like that, his smile didn't seem dingy anymore. Just brown.

"What?"

"I hate the fucking ocean."

He roared with laughter. I smiled, self-conscious, wishing I could muster a more generous response.

"Ever been to sea?" he asked.

"Uh uh."

"It never stops rolling." He made a waving motion with his hand. "First day out I puked my guts out. Then I puked some more. I couldn't stop puking. *Oh, you'll get used to it*, they told me. *You'll get your sea legs.* And maybe I would have, but the first port we called at I ran away."

"What do you mean, ran away?"

"I was still under contract, see? You can't just jump ship in the middle of a run. *Sorry. Not my cup of tea. See you later.* That sort of thing."

"But you did."

"Like your friend. It's the one with the blue eyes, isn't it?"

I nodded.

"Like her. I knew what I could take and what I couldn't."

He hesitated. I thought he might be about to reveal something extraordinary. Maybe some clue about what Gina could and couldn't take.

"So we get to Halifax and everyone's ribbing me about drinking and whoring. Gotta make a man of me, right?"

"I guess."

"So I go along with them, but not for what you think."

He waited in case I might want to fill in what I thought. I didn't, so he continued.

"To get away. And I didn't go around telling anyone beforehand. No one. Not even the Norski who'd taken me under his wing. Some way to return a favour, eh? But if I'd told him, you think I'd be sitting here now?"

I shook my head. He nodded.

"Your friend knows what she's about."

"How do you know?"

"I know her type," he said, not unkindly.

Easy, I thought as I went up to my apartment. All you have to do is ask a few questions, and look what you get. A conversation, if not necessarily the truth.

I opened my refrigerator and considered my options. There were two I could think of: spend the rest of the day, the year, my life shuttling between my living room and laundromat, hoping a hint of Gina's aura might waft by me, or force myself to keep asking questions. I had tried the first approach before, with my mother, with Lynn. I'd stayed where they'd left me, perfectly still, waiting for some part of them to drift back. When all that came my way were memories, fantasies, I grabbed those. I held them for years in the limbo of my imagination, as their real lives spun further and further from my reach. I was ready to try something else.

Gina's landlord was an obvious place to start, I thought, as I headed out the door. I should have gone to him right after speaking to Polly, maybe even before, but I never liked being around him. A twitchy guy, he was always wiping his nose with the back of his hands and talking to Gina's tits about investments, deals and the killings he was going to make. That's why he had bought Gina's house in the first place. To make a killing. Nothing wrong with that, I supposed, except that I didn't like it, didn't like how he looked at Gina, and didn't like how he looked at me either, dismissing me with a quick glance at my face and tits, flicking away like I was some kind of bad investment.

He did have good taste, though. The house where Gina lived, drab as a mushroom just a few days earlier, was now the colours of sunset. I stopped in my tracks as I approached. Two men were still painting it, applying a layer of flame over fungus. I had to admire it, no matter what I thought of her landlord. It was so bold, so perfect, I wondered who had ever made up the rule that orange and red clash.

I walked over. The painters didn't know if the landlord was home, they were just painting, what did I think? Nice, I told them, wishing I had a word to match their colours. "A bit much for me," one of them said as I watched the trim around the window come to life under his brush. I thought of the old oatmeal I'd applied to the walls of my laundromat. True, I'd been aiming for sand, but would sand have been that much better? These were the colours I should have chosen. Auburns, oranges, burning reds. Colours with enough muscle to punch through Vancouver's winter sky and drag out whatever light was hiding within. Although even as I thought that, objectors began to nag me: Marlene, on the run from too much muscle; Josie, huddled by her radiator, sinking comfortably into the blandness I offered.

The front door was open. I walked in, up the familiar wide staircase that wound to the top floor and Gina's closed door. I listened before I knocked. Silence, and silence again after I knocked. I tried the handle. It opened.

The place was empty. Lots of dust and crumbs on the unswept floors, but aside from that the tarnished gold dome above me was the only remaining sign of Gina. The apartment was small—just the one, domed room, a bathroom and kitchenette—and seemed smaller and more run down without Gina's pictures, fabrics and jewelry hanging everywhere, distracting. The plaster on the walls was cracked in some places, unevenly patched in others. There were water stains on the wall where Gina's huge maroon and gold tapestry had hung just days before. The floor was the best feature of the apartment. Old fir, it glowed red in the late afternoon sun. I sat on it, in a shaft of light slanting through the window, less to think things through than to absorb what I could, regain my bearings.

The sun reflected off the ceiling as well as the floor, suspended dust thickening its light. The whole place glowed with an unearthly sort of light. I remembered Gina telling me once that in another century she would have been a nun. I tried to remember why. Not confession—you didn't have to be a nun to go to confession, and that had been another of her lies anyway. Embellishments. She liked to claim that she learned the basics of her career in the confession booth, that the priests behind the curtain were her first, and remained her most appreciative, audience. "Coming up with a routine at Xandu's is nothing once you've spun a priest," she'd said, grinning. "I mean, you can't keep repeating yourself in confession, and you can't rely on visuals or anything . . ." I couldn't remember the rest. Didn't want to. It was Gina I was after, not another of her routines.

She had been to a convent school. That much, at least, was true. "Last stop before reform school," she'd explained, but had nothing bad to say about it.

"I've heard the nuns in those places can be weird," I'd said.

"No weirder than anyone else," she'd countered.

"And all the rules?"

Nothing compared to the rules in some of the homes she had lived in before.

"What about the masochism?" I asked.

"What masochism?"

"You know. All the self-denial stuff."

"That's not masochism," she'd answered. "That's love."

A sniffle interrupted my thoughts. I reeled around to see Gina's landlord standing in the doorway. Filling it.

"Help you with something?" he asked.

"I'm looking for Gina," I said, stupidly.

A crooked grin split his face then disappeared. "Having any luck?"

"When did she move her stuff out?" I asked, and when he didn't answer right away, I explained that she'd been missing since Wednesday, I was a friend of hers, I was worried, I had no idea where she was. "Did she give you notice?" I asked.

"You Tova?" he answered.

"How do you know?"

"I don't," he answered. "Wouldn't have to ask if I did, would I?" A slight twitch flicked one side of his mouth. Like a snake tongue, I thought, then made myself stop. "Gina said I'd recognize you," he said accusingly, as if it was my fault he didn't. His eyes narrowed a bit then wandered over me as if trying to locate some familiar landmark. He must have found it because he nodded, returned his eyes to mine and said, "She left some stuff for you." He gave his nose a quick wipe with his hand before extending the same hand to me. "I'm Jim, by the way."

I shook his hand. It was moist on both sides, but not slimy.

"So you interested in this stuff or not?" His shoulder jerked.

"What do you mean, 'stuff'? What kind of stuff?"

"Beats me." He shrugged, an exaggerated shrug, which I suspected was an attempt to camouflage the continued jerking of his shoulder. Nerves, illness or drugs had him short-circuited. I couldn't tell which. "It's just a few boxes."

I followed him down to his apartment. One of the painters was in the stairwell, beginning to scrape off the pale peeling green that had once coated the bannister.

"Repainting the inside too?" I asked Jim.

He didn't answer, might have thought I was talking to the painter.

"The outside looks great."

Still no response. That was unexpected. Anytime I'd seen him before, he had rattled non-stop to Gina about his big plans for the place, all his muscles jerking, pulled by invisible strings, as he built up to his grand finale: the killing he was going to make when he finally sold the dump. I guessed I just wasn't his type.

We walked the rest of the way downstairs in silence and when we got to his apartment he wordlessly held the door open so I could see the three cardboard boxes stacked inside. Each one had my name scrawled across it in thick black ink.

"Where's the rest of her stuff?" I asked.

"Beats me," he said, various parts of him beginning to twitch. Something about Gina's boxes obviously pulled at his nerves. Maybe just being in their presence. His twitching continued as we stood there silently. His eyes slid down to my chin, then to my chest. I wondered if his tit-staring was less a matter of lust than an attempt to find a comfortable resting place for nervous eyes. I decided I was being too generous.

"So you going to take this or not?" he asked.

"Yeah, sure. I just have to figure out how to get it home. I don't have a car."

He shrugged a "Not my problem" kind of shrug and wiped his nose with his wrist.

"Can I come back and get them tonight?"

"I'm busy tonight."

I didn't even want to imagine with what.

"I can't hold them forever," he added, which was how I ended up spending the rest of the afternoon shuttling them by foot, one at a time, back to my apartment.

On my last trip I asked again if Gina had given him notice.

"She's paid up until the end of the month."

I assumed, since he was releasing her property to me, that that was enough notice for Jim.

"Did she move the rest of her stuff out herself?" I asked.

"Beats me," he said, drumming his fingers against the door he was itching to close on me.

"She say where she was going?"

"What are you, her mother or something?"

"I'm just trying to figure out where she might have gone."

"Beats me," he said again.

I knew I should persist, insist, was trying to think of a follow-up question as the door clicked shut in my face. I'm not good in a clutch, I thought as I tried to find a comfortable way to carry the box. I have no knack for anything which requires quick-on-your-feet responses and getting things right the first time around. Like life.

The third box was the heaviest by far. I had to stop every few feet to shift it, put it down on the sidewalk to rest my arms. It was close to 5:00 by the time I got it safely home. I still hadn't thought up a snappy response to Jim, the magic question that would unleash his torrent of helpful information. I was hungry, tired, had no groceries in the house and was craving tea. A person up to the task of finding Gina would ignore all that, I told myself, and tear into the three boxes that now stood by the foot of my bed.

I opened the box I had just put down. It was filled with books. Heavy books. I pulled one out—*Black Beauty* in hardcover—then another, *The Bible*, King James version. Next out was *The Story of O*. Also hardcover. *Loretta Mason Potts*; a dog-eared *Lives of the Saints*; *Two Lives and a Dream*, by Marguerite Yourcenar; a few mysteries, American mostly; *Jane Eyre* and *Jane Eyre* again.

I opened the other two boxes, both considerably smaller and lighter than the first. One was filled with trinkets—costume jewelry, a few animal figurines she'd had staring out of various corners of her apartment, several candleholders, an amazing assortment of candles, and her bag of different bird feathers she'd found around the city. The other had her box collection, wood and glass boxes, some of which she had kept on her night table, others which I'd never seen before.

No doubt there was a clue in all of this, but I was too hungry to try to figure it out. Dizzy. I thought of the mystery I'd just finished, of the P.I.—female, at that—who didn't eat, sleep, wash or drink anything but scotch and coffee until she got to the bottom of her case. Didn't seem to, anyway. Maybe she did and it just didn't make it into the story. Maybe she ate three times a day, and stopped in at the dry-cleaners and had a cleaning woman come in once a week, but those parts got cut, along with all the people who cooked the unmentioned meals, and cleaned the expensive, well-described clothes, and tidied all the messes she had to have made. People like me.

I repacked Gina's boxes and shoved them under the bed—I don't know why, maybe a touch of drama to offset the mundane tasks I was about to do—then set out on my errands. It was dark already. I walked quickly toward Chinatown to get all my shopping done before the stores closed. I bought my groceries in record time and made it to the tea shop just as the saleswoman was locking up. She unlocked it with a nod—I'd been coming there every Sunday afternoon for two years.

"White Peony?" she asked.

I nodded, then changed my mind. "You have any Cliff Monkey?"

If she was shocked she didn't show it. Maybe ordering something different wasn't such a shocking thing to some people. "You don't like Cliff Monkey," she said.

That was true. She'd introduced me to it a few months back. A beautiful tea, the colour of honey, its flavour was too pungent for my taste.

"I thought I would give it another try," I said. It was its story I was after, not its flavour. She'd told me that it was a tea that grew so high on cliffs, so far out of people's reach, that monkeys had to be sent up to pick it. "Maybe I'll develop a taste for it."

"Very expensive," she said.

"How expensive?"

"Very."

Too expensive for my budget, it turned out. She sold me enough for two cups, along with my weekly supply of White Peony. As I was leaving the store, she wished me good luck. I turned around, about to ask her *Good luck with what?* but decided wishes like that were better left open-ended.

9

Gina's belongings were no more revealing
on a full stomach. She had left no note, no explanation, no indication of what I was supposed to do with it all, and for how long.
Still I kept sifting through the boxes, shaking books for the note I
might have missed, the clues she hadn't left.

I opened *Two Lives and a Dream*, and stared at the titles of the
stories for a while. "An Obscure Man," "A Lovely Morning," "Anna
Soror" . . . So what, I wondered as I started leafing through the
pages. There was an iris pressed into the middle of "An Obscure
Man." I remembered the vivid blues and violets of the irises she
had once brought me. This one was limp, faded and beginning to
brown along its edges. I replaced it carefully, sadly, half sorry I'd
disturbed its resting place, then closed the book.

I was surprised to see "Property of Vancouver School Board"
stamped inside one copy of *Jane Eyre*, with Gina's name and grade
7B printed neatly beside it. Anything she had told me about her
life before fifteen had been set in the Prairies, Winnipeg mostly.
But then, she had also told me she'd moved around, grown up "all
over," and what difference did it make anyway? I repacked the
books, disappointed, and turned to the next carton.

Her feather collection took up the top third of it. A large plastic
bag filled with pigeon feathers, I pulled it out carefully, afraid it
might carry some kind of disease. The two feathers that had

actually seemed worth collecting—the hawk feather, the white tuft from a snowy owl—were missing. Their absence irritated me. Whatever else had been going on for Gina before she left, she had obviously had the time and presence of mind to pluck out from her life what was rare, lucky or beautiful and take it with her. Leaving me the pigeon feathers.

Wedged in the middle of that carton, among her beaded earrings, glass necklaces, candles and animal figurines, was the crucifix that had hung on her wall. Graphic to the point of gruesome, it was, she had told me, from one of the classrooms at her convent.

"You stole a crucifix from a convent?" I asked.

"I didn't *steal* it," she assured me. "I was the only one it meant anything to."

"How old were you?"

"When?" As if she had lost track of the conversation we were having.

"When it meant something to you."

"It still does. Fifteen."

"It's a bit gruesome," I pointed out. It was the bloodiest crucifix I'd ever laid eyes on.

"I know." She smiled.

"So why do you keep it?" And on the wall directly across from her bed, so it would be the first thing she saw whenever she opened her eyes.

"As a reminder."

I waited.

"That style is everything. In suffering as in everything else."

I looked for the glint in her eye, the sign that she was pulling me along, leading me somewhere I hadn't been, hadn't even considered. She was propped against the pillows of her bed, facing me, her eyes on the crucifix.

"So you saw that at fifteen and decided . . ."

She shook her head. "I saw that at fifteen and missed the point. I thought it meant that not everyone gets to suffer, that you have to be chosen for it. Special."

I nodded, though she still wasn't looking at me. "So . . ."

"Six months in the bin," she said, holding out her hands to me, palms down. I'd already noticed the scars, one small circle of white on the back of each hand. I'd assumed they were cigarette burns, had decided not to ask. "I used a chisel," she said.

"You did that? To yourself?"

"I got the idea in woodworking class. It seemed right. At the time, anyway."

"No wonder they locked you up."

"Exactly." She nodded. "The wrong style. You can't go around piercing your hands. Your ears, nose, lips, tits, tongue—Christ, you can even do your clit."

"Labia."

She held her hands in front of her face and shook her head. "Hands and feet make people nervous."

I put the crucifix back, remembering how I had tried to believe her, tried to be carried along, but was unable. The little white circles were too clearly burns, cigarette burns—I felt disloyal for knowing. I had tried to follow her words, to imagine her, ecstatic, as she chiselled the skin on her hands, but, in the end, I betrayed her. The circles were burned into her skin by somebody else, I couldn't help knowing. Long before she ever saw Jesus suffering stylishly on the cross. And for no more exalted or interesting reason than to stop her from crying. Or to make her cry. Or for no reason at all.

I turned to the next carton—her collection of small boxes. Most were empty. One held a few marbles, which she'd fried until they split with a million internal hairline fractures. I'd also done that as a kid, ruined my entire marble collection in one night just for the momentary pleasure of watching them split apart beneath their undisturbed surfaces. A small black velvet box near the bottom of the carton held a simple gold cross on a thin chain that must have hung around her neck sometime before Terry's choker.

At the bottom of the carton was a flat, carved wooden box filled with locks of hair, each one tied with a string. Gina had told me once about a woman she knew who saved a lock of hair from each lover. I had said that was disgusting. It was less disgusting than weird, I thought now, and wondered why she couldn't have just saved a note from each, a photo, a valentine, an article of clothing.

In among the locks was a newspaper clipping about the acquittal of a man in Victoria, ten years earlier, on charges of rape and child procurement, and another clipping about the murder of the same man, also in Victoria, two years later, in a fight outside a bar. I already knew Gina had been raped, though I'd thought it had happened more recently. "A few years ago," she'd said when she told me. "The prick," she'd added in a tone that made me wonder if she'd known him beforehand. When I asked she said, "Not really."

I hadn't realized she had reported it to the police, much less gone to trial and lost. And I didn't know he was dead. Murdered. When I'd asked her if she watched over her shoulder for him she'd shrugged. "Not really," she said. "He's the one who should be watching his back," she added a little later, when I thought we'd already moved on to another conversation.

She hadn't said anything about a child being involved. More than one, according to the article. I reread the article a few times, trying to piece together the connection between the rape and the child procurement charges, but couldn't. As I put the clipping back among the locks of hair, I wondered why she would include an article about her rapist among the momentoes from her lovers, a man who had forced himself on her among those she'd welcomed. Presumably.

I found myself dialling Marlene's number, Gina's belongings still strewn all around me. Before I'd figured out why I was calling or what I would say, she answered, her voice hesitant, wheedling. Fear, I thought, and wondered if it was possible Gabe was already back outside her window.

"Marlene?"

"Oh it's you," she exhaled. "Hi."

"What's the matter?"

"Oh, you know." She sounded confused.

"Is he back?" What I had wanted was conversation, I realized, a human voice, the reassurance of it.

"No. Not really. I mean, he's not outside."

"Where is he?"

"I don't know. He's taken to calling me now."

"What's he saying?"

"Nothing. He just calls."

"How often?"

"Oh, every half-hour, give or take."

"He calls you every half-hour and says nothing?"

She didn't answer.

"Does he breathe into the phone?"

"No. Nothing. He just calls." Normally Marlene would be irritated at having to repeat herself three times. Tonight she didn't seem to notice.

"I thought the police picked him up," I said.

"They did. They couldn't hold him, though. I only have a family court restraining order. I guess I need a peace bond for them to hold him."

"You guess?" I was the one getting irritated. There was something about the exhaustion in her voice, the resignation. I wanted her to fight, get back at him, do what I wouldn't be able to do in her situation, couldn't seem to do in any situation: rise to it, transform it.

"So how do you go about getting a peace bond?" I asked.

"We have to have another hearing. My lawyer set it up for tomorrow. Though she's not sure . . . see, he's never actually been dangerously violent toward me. He's just . . ."

"So what, they have to wait until he's actually tried to kill you or something?" There was a moment's silence before Marlene reminded me that Gabriel had rights too and since he hadn't actually hit her, had only thrown a dozen eggs at her, which isn't really considered dangerously violent . . .

"Why don't you take your phone off the hook for the rest of the night?" I asked, fighting off the image of Marlene crouched, braced against the next egg, yolk sliding off her face and hair.

"What for?" she asked.

"So you can get some sleep, for one thing."

"If the line's busy he might get mad."

"That's crazy," I said, then regretted it. Who was I . . . ? "It's not crazy, Marlene," I said. "It's just . . . Can I do anything?" I finally thought to ask.

"Oh, that's OK, Tova. It's nice that you called. It really means a lot to me." The words sounded flimsy, empty, as if there was only a scrap of Marlene left in them.

"Do you want me to come over?"

"No sense both of us losing a night's sleep. Someone's got to be awake for work tomorrow."

"I guess," I agreed too quickly, too relieved that I had offered and been turned down. I'd done what I could, I thought, as I put the phone down. I made myself the cup of tea I'd been craving all evening and drank it, surrounded by the contents of Gina's cartons, the remnants of yet another relationship in which I'd gone halfway. I repacked Gina's boxes and called Marlene back.

"I'm coming over," I said.

"You don't need to," she offered.

"I know, but I want to." She didn't turn me down.

"It seems to me that what's in Gina's cartons isn't as important as what you hope is in them," Marlene said softly.

We were sitting in her kitchen. I had told her everything, at least everything I could put into words.

"See, what you're really looking for is yourself. That's what we're all looking for: ourselves."

"Please, Marlene," I said, sorry I had told her. "You may be looking for yourself, but I'm looking for Gina."

I should never have brought it up, I realized. Marlene had never really talked to Gina, but obviously didn't like her. The descriptions of Xandu's had disgusted her, I could see it on her face: her lips delicately pursed, her colour slightly heightened. She was the last person I should have confided in, revealed Gina to.

"Maybe I should read that story she marked," I said. "The one the flower was in."

"What for?" Marlene asked.

I shrugged.

"You could," Marlene said doubtfully. "But it all seems pretty gamey to me. I mean, it just doesn't seem like Gina really wants you to know what she's about. Not just you, Tova. Anyone."

I knew that wasn't true. "Why would she have sent me all this stuff if she didn't want me to . . . ?" To what, I wondered. I felt

certain that Gina was trying to tell me something, point me somewhere. Unfortunately, I couldn't figure out what or where. Or—
apart from wearing Terry's choker—what to do.

There was a short silence while Marlene searched for a bland
way to tell me I was a jerk. That was the most noticeable change
in her since she'd started her counselling. She dipped her thoughts
in vanilla before letting them out of her mouth.

"A lot of women make the same mistake you're making," Marlene
said. "We see someone who has no regard for us and think he just
doesn't know how to express it. We see inconsideration and think
it's poor communication skills. We see . . . "

I wished she would drop the "we," like this was some kind of
kindergarten I had accidentally enrolled in.

"What we can't seem to accept is that we can't—"

The phone rang. We both froze, looked at each other. A second
ring, and she rose to get it. A few seconds of silence followed her
hello. She turned her back to me, picked up a pencil that was lying
on the counter and stuck the eraser in and out of the telephone dial.
"Is that you, Gabe?" she asked finally, her voice soft, more careful
than frightened. More silence, then, "I'm going to put the phone
down now," which she did.

"Asshole," I said when she returned to the table. She didn't
agree or disagree.

"I thought I would heat up some apple cider," she said. "Would
you like some?"

I said I would and watched her move around her kitchen,
pulling cinnamon sticks out of one glass jar, cloves out of another,
and a small gingham-wrapped bundle of spices from a basket
hanging near the telephone. The kitchen was tiny, standard, the
kind found in every low-rise in the neighbourhood, my own
included, but Marlene had remade it into a theme-park vision—or

maybe her own—of cozy. Yellow gingham covered the table, framed the window, and turned up again in the tea towels and the cozies that covered the appliances lining the counter. The walls were the colour of butter, bordered at the top with blue geese and red hearts, and checkered with framed samplers of little girls in kerchiefs chasing butterflies or contemplating rainbows. And all around, on ledges, and hanging from the wall and ceiling, were baskets filled with dried flowers, herbs and fruit.

Marlene saw me taking it in. "I tried to make it nice. For the kids, you know. This has been so hard on them."

"It's really nice," I managed, wondering if her first kitchen after she married had been like this, or if she had worked up to it gradually, as real domestic coziness inched further and further out of reach.

I watched her as she stood by the stove stirring the cider. I had expected her to look as worn as her voice had sounded over the phone, her hair to hang lank and oily, her eyes to be dull, but she looked the same as usual: a layer of rosy makeup, her lips glossy and pink, her hair freshly washed and pulled into a high ponytail. A cheerleader's ponytail, I thought. She wore a pink sweatsuit and plush white slippers that made her feet look like small rabbits.

"It was sweet of you to come over like this," she said, and I wondered if sweet was what she was aiming for—always, with every softened sentence, fluffy fabric and hint of lavender that wafted from her skin and hair. "It's easier with you here." She poured our cider into mugs as I tried to think of a response—*I'm glad? I'm happy to be here?* I was, oddly. Relieved to be away from the scattered bits of Gina that littered my apartment.

Marlene handed me my mug of cider and sat down opposite me. I took a sip. It wasn't as cloying as I had feared. I was still trying to think of something to say. She stood up, leaned over to my side of the table and unhooked the white lace that held the curtain open. It fell closed, then she closed her side.

"Is that where he sits?" I asked, indicating the window, the vague dark space beyond it, suddenly nervous about who might be watching us from the street below.

"Sometimes. When he's not calling me every half-hour. Though he could be calling me from a car phone for all I know. Watching me get up, answer the phone: 'Is that you, Gabe?' " Her imitation of the voice she used with Gabe was perfect, surprising me. "I'm sure that would be a real kick for him."

I wondered if he was out there now, watching as we sat by the lit window, curtained only in flimsy yellow gingham, drinking cider.

"Do you think we should move away from the window?" I asked, just in case Marlene hadn't yet considered the possibility that he could be on his way over with a shotgun. But she obviously had. She nodded immediately.

We grabbed our mugs and padded down the dark carpeted hallway, past a shut door where I assumed her kids were sleeping, to an alcove with no window. There was a couch—a hide-a-bed—with lamps on either side and a long narrow coffee table in front of it. She turned on the lamps and we sat on the couch facing the dark hallway.

"You read this yet?" she asked, pointing to one of the books on the coffee table. *Women Who Run with the Wolves.*

"Uh uh." Gina had. She'd sworn it had changed her life, but couldn't say how, exactly.

"Oh, you have to," Marlene said, reaching for it.

"My great-grandmother was eaten by wolves," I said.

"She was?"

"Yeah. Back in Russia." I had been told that growing up, had only recently begun to suspect that she might have run off with the wolf voluntarily. Like her granddaughter did, fifty years later. My mother. "I guess it was pretty common back then. For Jews anyway. That's why a lot of Jews are afraid of dogs."

"They are?"

I don't know why I said it, any of it. Maybe to stop her from finding her favourite passage and reading it out loud to me. Gina had already read me half the book. All of it seemed to be her favourite passage. I realized now that it wasn't in among the books she had left with me.

The phone rang. Marlene answered, repeated what she had done the last time he called. She replaced the receiver quietly.

"Why are you being so nice to him?" I asked. I wanted her to blow a whistle in his ear, to deafen and scare him to death at the same time. Or to come up with something worse, better, something I didn't have the imagination to consider.

"I don't want to provoke him."

"You don't want to provoke . . . ?"

"I can handle him calling like this."

"But every half-hour?"

"At least I can keep track of him this way. If I can keep him satisfied with this tonight, keep him away from us, tomorrow I can get my peace bond and change my phone number."

I hadn't thought of that, changing her phone number. I don't know why. I should have.

"So where were we?" Marlene asked.

We both thought for a moment.

"Your books," I remembered.

"My books," she repeated absentmindedly, distracted now.

I waited, but she didn't go on. I wondered if Gabe was getting to her more than she was letting on. All evening she had seemed cooler than I would have expected, more in control. I kept waiting for her to break down, for her voice to unravel at the end of every word, but until now it hadn't.

"There's something I have to tell you," she said after a long silence. Her whole tone had shifted. Her voice was lower than I had ever heard it. "This Roger . . ."

I waited. I had suspected I'd shocked her when I told her about him, about all my encounters at Xandu's. I'd been expecting some sort of lecture.

"He's a pimp, Tova."

"No kidding," I said.

"I mean he's really bad news."

I wondered where she got off, Miss Gingham, with her rabbit feet and three sleeping children, educating me on subtleties about pimps.

"I think you need to be a lot more careful than you've been."

"Careful how?" *What would you know?* is what I meant.

"From what you've told me, Roger doesn't seem to see himself for what he is. I mean it's pretty obvious that he's just your basic run-of-the-mill pimp, but for some reason he seems to think he isn't, that he's, like, some kind of saviour or something. People like that who can't see what or who they are can be dangerous."

I nodded. She'd pegged him there. The first person I'd talked to who shared my instinct about him, who didn't say, *Roger's not so bad.* "The way Lois tells it, he's doing his girls a big favour," I said. "It's like one big happy family to him."

"And Lois is, what did you figure, sixteen? seventeen? That's what he relies on, I bet. Kids. Kids with no place to go, no money, no skills, no way to support themselves, no idea that there are things you can have without having to fuck for them, things you can do with your life besides fucking your way through it."

I had never heard Marlene use language like that.

"So how am I not being careful enough?" I asked.

She leaned toward me from her end of the couch. Crouching forward like that, feet pulled under her, she looked like a sorority girl about to reveal the secret of which boy she had a crush on.

"If you want to look for Gina, I think you're going to have to learn to keep your mouth shut a little more. Keep your opinions more to yourself. Know what I mean?"

Stung, I shook my head.

"Well, it seems, you know, from listening to what you've told me, that Gina isn't really missing. It sounds to me like she's just watching her back. And from everything you've said, it sounds like it's Roger she's watching for." She paused to make sure I was following. "So probably you shouldn't be going around telling everyone what you're thinking about where she might be, or showing people, even telling them about what she sends you. You know, like her cartons and stuff, that choker you're wearing." She paused again. I nodded. "Because, you don't really know how wide his net is, right?" I nodded again. "And let's say there's something you're missing, some message or something she's trying to send to you and you're missing it for some reason, anybody you tell can pick it up and follow it right to her. Know what I mean?"

I was so humiliated I couldn't speak.

"See, because everything you say to Lois goes directly back to Roger. Everything. Know what I mean?"

"How do you know?" I asked. "What makes you so sure Roger—"

She cut me off. "People who can't see who they really are are dangerous," she repeated.

"But don't you think most people can't—"

"Like Gabe," she continued, as if I hadn't tried to interrupt. "Mr.

Mellow. Your classic aging hippie. As long as I went along with the scene, baking his bread, cooking his meals, sewing his clothes, typing and editing all his manuscripts, popping out his kids—no anaesthetic, of course, that would be unnatural—everything was fine. Things were basically OK between us . . . I mean, he didn't actually start getting mean with me until I pointed out he was a controlling bastard." She paused. "And I bet that's what happened between Gina and Roger. I bet what happened is Gina started seeing him for what he is."

"Roger isn't Gabe," I said.

Marlene shrugged. "He's worse."

"How would you know?" I asked.

"My bet is Gina finally saw Roger for what he is and told him off. She's pretty mouthy, isn't she?"

"She is, but this isn't some little domestic drama, Marlene. I mean, I hardly see Gina running away just because she told Roger off. I realize Gabe . . ." I stopped because Marlene was tugging at the neckline of her sweatshirt. She pulled it down far enough to reveal a thick white scar that stretched across her chest.

"That's what happens when you tell people like him what they really are."

"I'm sorry," I said. It felt meagre. I hadn't realized. Four years I'd worked with her, on and off, had actually waved at Gabe when he dropped her off at work. More than once. "When did he do that to you?"

"Roger did this to me," she said, and covered herself again.

"Roger? How do you know—"

"This isn't about me," she cut me off.

I waited for her to go on, but she didn't. I had to know how she knew Roger. I asked again. "That's not the point," she said. "The point is Gina." She paused, then said, "It seems to me that Gina finally got it together to get clear of Roger. So if you really care about her, Tova . . ."

"How do you know Roger?" I asked again.

"Knew," she said. "I worked for him once. Briefly." She smiled. "Though not briefly enough. But it was a while ago, Tova. Honestly."

I could see that. The scar was old, faded.

"And my past really isn't the point here. The point is Gina."

I nodded numbly, heard her repeat that it seemed Gina had finally gotten it together . . .

"I'm not sure it's that simple," I said.

Marlene shook her head. "Things don't have to be complicated."

"There's something else going on besides Gina finally noticing that Roger's a pig."

"Like what?" Marlene wasn't buying it. I could hear it in her tone, see it in her face and the way she sat with her arms folded across her chest.

"I don't know yet," I admitted.

Marlene snorted, then shook her head. "What this is about, Tova, is one guy's ego."

The phone rang. I didn't even hear how Marlene handled it this time. When she got off the phone she was trembling so much it was hard to pretend I didn't notice.

"What did he say?" I asked.

"Nothing."

I looked at my watch. Exactly 1:00 A.M. "He's persistent," I said.

Marlene's mouth twisted into a thin line that could have been a grimace or a smile. "In some things," she agreed, then she shook her head as if to clear it. "Where were we?" she asked.

"Roger," I said. "What Gina might be running from."

Marlene nodded.

"Don't you find it a bit strange how many teenaged girls seem to orbit around Roger?" I asked.

Marlene shrugged. "I'm not saying Roger's not up to his eyeballs in sleaze. Sure he's dealing in kids. That's a given with him. He was dealing in kids fifteen years ago."

"Is that when you knew him?" I asked.

"That isn't what this thing with Gina is about," Marlene went on. "Gina crossed him personally. Mark my words."

"Apple or raisin?" George asked, but he

was looking at my neck.

"Apple, to go." I glanced at my watch. "And a cup of coffee for here."

Later than usual, I had missed George's morning rush. Half the tables were empty, everybody already at work. Just two sips of coffee, I told myself.

"So where'd you get it?" George asked when he brought my coffee.

"What?" I asked.

"That." He was staring at my neck.

"From Gina." I poured cream into my coffee, stirred in sugar, took my first sip.

"Don't play games with me," he said, an edge in his voice I had heard before, but never directed at me. He'd never been angry at me before, I realized. Strange to know someone as long as I'd known George and never inspire anger, never inspire anything more than gossip and wisecracks, and the occasional bit of fond concern.

"Who's playing games?" I asked. I kept sipping at the coffee. I didn't think I'd ever tasted coffee quite so good, quite so strong, creamy and sweet at the same time.

"Where the hell did you get that?" he asked.

I put the cup down. "Are you swearing at me, George?"

He gripped his edge of the counter with both hands. For a second I thought he might lift it, upend the whole counter and send coffee, knives, plates and glasses flying in my direction.

"What's with you this morning?" he asked, his bushy eyebrows raised. The image of George as Terminator dissolved as suddenly as it had appeared. He looked tired. He was leaning against the counter, I realized, not gripping its edge.

"Nothing," I said. A bald lie. I was also tired. Exhausted. I had spent a whole weekend trying to track Gina down and everything I'd tried had only made her cloudier in my mind, pushed her further out of reach. "I'm really worried about Gina," I said.

"Have you seen her?" George asked.

"She sent this to me. In the mail." I was about to go into the whole story—the odd packaging, the cryptic note, the cartons she'd left for me at her apartment—when I remembered Marlene's warning. I glanced around George's half-filled café wondering who was within earshot, who might be interested enough in Gina's whereabouts to be listening. According to Marlene, everyone was suspect. *Vancouver's a small town,* she had said at one point in the night when I was still expressing my shock that she knew Roger. Had known him at one time anyway. *Smaller than you'd think,* she had said. Even George could be another direct line to Roger, I supposed. I looked at his face, its familiar combination of open and wary. I had known him for years now, had trusted him the first moment I met him.

"She mailed it to you?" George asked. "From where?"

I shrugged.

"Well, what did the postmark say?"

Vancouver, I remembered. I shrugged again. "I don't know. I didn't check."

"You trying to tell me you're worried sick about Gina, something comes from her in the mail, and you didn't check the postmark?"

Caught, I could only attack. "I haven't noticed you sharing any information with me," I said.

"What are you talking about?"

"If anyone's been playing games about this, it's you. Acting coy, telling me Gem's 'real' name is something you just somehow picked up along the way, telling me Gina's been looking for Gem without telling me how you know."

"What do you want to know?" George asked. His quiet, serious tone was another side of him I hadn't seen very often.

"How you know Gem's real name."

Rumour, I expected him to say. Gossip. He poured himself a cup of coffee. For a second I thought he might actually drink it.

"That's the name the cops used when they came around asking for her. Gem's just a nickname."

"An alias?"

George smiled. "I think it's just a nickname."

"What else did they say?"

"Nothing." He met my eye. "When the cops come by they're not generally the ones who do the talking."

I nodded, appreciating what it took for George to admit that to me.

"So how did you figure out she might be connected to the man in the dumpster?"

"Rumour. Really," he said, meeting my eye again.

I believed him. Marlene had come into work that same day with the same rumour hot in her mouth. Like an out-of-control fire, I thought, a rumour like that.

"Who do you think started it?" I asked.

"Now there's a question," George said, pointing his spoon at me. He stirred his coffee, but still didn't drink it.

"So what about this business about Gina looking for Gem. Who started that one?"

"That wasn't a rumour," he said. "Gina asked me if I had heard anything about where Gem might be."

"Gina," I repeated. "Why would she ask *you?*"

He smiled. "I do overhear things."

"When did she ask you?"

"Tuesday night," he said. The night before she'd taken off. The night I'd gone home to read a mystery and eat a cheese sandwich.

"What did she want with Gem?"

George wrapped his hands around his coffee cup, shrugged.

"Did you ask her?"

"Of course I asked her. She said Gem had something of hers she needed back. Some photo."

"A photo," I repeated. "Of what?"

"Of Gina."

"Where would Gem get a photo of Gina? What kind of photo?"

George shrugged again. "It was just your standard photo, far as I know."

"And that's why she had to find Gem right at the second the cops are also looking for her?"

George nodded.

"Jesus," I said. "Couldn't she have come up with something a little better than that? I mean, did she expect you to believe that?" The arrogance of it.

George didn't answer. He was staring into his coffee now.

"You didn't believe her, did you?"

He still didn't answer. He wouldn't even look at me.

"How could you have? *Why* would you? I mean, given the circumstances. Not to mention Gina's peculiar relationship to the truth."

"Gina didn't lie to me," he said quietly.

That's when I noticed he'd shaved his beard.

"Your beard," I started to say.

It was the way he brought his hand up to his face, as if to cover anything else I might notice, that made me understand.

"Were you and Gina lovers?" I asked. Not a word I had ever used with George. We had joked plenty about who was getting it. Action. Never love.

He met my eye again, but didn't answer.

"Since when?" I asked.

"A while."

How long a while, I wondered, and why, once again, had no one told me?

"So were you two ever planning on telling me, or were you just going to sneak around until I figured it out? Maybe drop me a postcard from Las Vegas?" I'd tried for a light tone but fallen miserably short. George could have told me it was none of my business, but he didn't. He smiled, a bit sadly, I thought, maybe kindly, and said, "It wasn't like that."

Like what? I wanted to ask.

"You know Gina," he said. I was less and less sure that I did. "She's private about that sort of thing."

I nodded, relieved that at least one other person understood Gina as private. He looked at me for a minute, his mind obviously miles away, then shook his head and said, "I had no idea she was taking off."

Another thing he and I shared in common.

"Are you worried?" I asked, not realizing I was expecting denial until he nodded. I had thought he would laugh, say something along the lines that he pitied anyone who would try to mess with Gina, but his face as he nodded was worried. I remembered why I had liked George from the first minute we met, the way he met my eye without turning it into a challenge, took me in without devouring me, released me without dismissing me. My instincts about people might be off, horrible even, but they were all I had.

"The postmark was Vancouver," I said.

"Hmm?"

"The postmark. On the package the choker came in."

"Vancouver," he repeated. He looked so miserable, I felt I should try to reassure him, offer some hope if not quite a promise that Gina was OK.

"It's probably a good sign that she sent me this," I said.

"How do you figure?"

"She's obviously still alive."

George didn't look relieved. "Hold on," he said, as if I would rush off while he went to take care of a few customers who had come in.

"So don't you think?" I asked when he came back.

"Don't I think what?" he asked as he reached over to run his finger along the edge of the choker. The light pressure of his touch, the shock of his finger as it grazed the skin on my neck—I pulled away.

"That it's a good sign. This arriving from her."

"No," he said, dropping his hand. "I don't think it's a good sign."

"It's raining," Josie greeted me.

"Could be worse," I said, and by noon it probably would be. A new front was moving in; we were still at the edge of it. A light drizzle was beginning to fall, still soft, but within a few hours there would be lots more rain, sheets of it. I was extremely tired.

I unlocked the door and made coffee for Josie. She didn't even look at me as she grabbed the mug from my hands. She brought it up to her face and started gulping. I watched her for a while, then counted the till over and over until my mind finally harnessed itself to the numbers my voice kept repeating. Eight-thirty, and only three customers. I swept the floor, though Marlene had left the place spotless. Then I reswept. I kept sweeping, the movements familiar and soothing. Josie was beginning to slurp at her empty coffee cup.

Vancouver's a small town kept repeating in my mind. I followed it: Marlene's voice, last night, when my shock and confusion were rearing up against what she was telling me about Roger. "It makes no sense," was all I could respond.

"What is it that makes no sense?" she had finally asked.

"That you would know Roger, for one thing."

"Vancouver's a small town," she had said. "Smaller than you'd think." And then what? I couldn't remember.

I kept sweeping, noticed the small patch of tar someone had tracked in over the summer. I'd been meaning to scrape it off for months.

And the trade in kids is smaller still, I remembered. *Ten, maybe fifteen percent of total trade. No more than that. Anyone who's involved in it gets to know the major players pretty quick.*

I asked her if she knew Gina. She looked confused.

"I just thought if you both were . . ."

"You mean back then?" she asked. "Did I know Gina back then?"

I nodded.

Marlene managed a smile. "Gina would have been a bit young

fifteen years ago, even by Roger's standards." She looked at me oddly. "How old do you think Gina is?"

Gina had never actually told me her age. Strange, maybe, but certainly not the strangest aspect of our relationship. It had simply never come up. "Thirty?"

"Try twenty-three or twenty-four. Twenty-five tops."

I'd thought about it but couldn't agree. It was true Gina took care of her skin, did those purifying fasts, tried to exercise, but she still couldn't pass for twenty-five. "I know she looks good . . ." I started to say.

"She doesn't look good," Marlene interrupted, without a hint of an attempt at sweetness. "She looks like shit. To tell you the truth, Tova, the first time I saw you talking to her, I thought to myself, there's a girl who'll be lucky to make it to thirty."

Stunned, unable to reply, I had scanned my memory for an image of Gina to check if what Marlene was saying could possibly be true. I told her about the newspaper clipping. "If you're right about her age, then she would only have been fourteen or fifteen when she was raped. There was nothing in the article about her being that young." Although there was the bit about child procurement. I didn't mention it. "And there's no way her rapist would have gotten off if she were."

Which was the point at which Marlene called me naive. Incredibly naive. Her sweet tone of voice in full force again, she explained that rape is hard to prove in court—I guess she assumed from the rest of our conversation that that's something I wouldn't have figured out for myself yet. "And it's even more difficult for prostitutes to prove."

"Gina's not a prostitute," I said. One point, at least, that I was sure about. Gina had said more than once that she couldn't imagine having to fuck the men who watched her, but that, on the other hand, some of her hooker friends couldn't imagine having to take off their clothes in front of a whole roomful of men. *To each her own, right?* she'd concluded and I'd agreed.

"She may not be now," Marlene said, "but she was at one point. And not working out of some place like Roger runs, from the looks of her. I would say she spent a good long time on the street."

"Gina wasn't working the streets at fifteen," I informed Marlene. Marlene raised her eyebrows, unevenly plucked, I noticed for the first time. "She was in a convent," I explained.

Marlene nodded, brought her eyebrows down. "Right," she said. "And I'm Joan of Arc."

"Cops came by," Josie said.

"Oh yeah?"

Josie nodded. "Two officers."

I had heard about her two officers before. Usually they came by to investigate the poisoning of her cat, though at times they were more interested in getting to the bottom of the dead pigeons. I wasn't sure, just yet, which dead pigeons.

"More coffee?" I asked. It was as slow a morning at the laundromat as it had been at George's. I wondered if there was a holiday everyone else was celebrating that no one had told me and Josie about. Josie was holding her empty mug out in front of her. I went to fill it.

Maybe I was going about this all wrong, I thought. Talking to other people, picking brains other than my own, as if they somehow had more knowledge about Gina than I did, as if anyone else's version of Gina was necessarily truer than mine. Maybe I already knew everything I needed to in order to find her, and all I had to do was acknowledge it and follow her tracks.

I called Polly.

"I was just about to call you," she said. "Any word?"

"No," I told her.

"I'm afraid I didn't call the police," Polly confessed before I had a chance to ask. "I thought about it, but I guess I felt maybe we were overreacting. I mean, not showing up for work for a few days is hardly . . ." Her voice trailed off.

"It's OK," I said, but it wasn't. Polly should have told me if she wasn't going to follow through. Two more days had gone by. Precious days.

"And it's not like we're family or anything," Polly went on. "For all we know, she's with her family right now. It's not really our place to call the police."

"Gina has no family," I said, immediately regretting it. Polly already felt superior to Gina, secure in her belief that only women like Gina disappeared, women who, through some fault Polly didn't share, couldn't make a decent life for themselves.

A few days was all it had taken Polly to shrug Gina off, shrug the whole situation off as nothing but a case of an ex-employee with sticky fingers. I knew that's how it went. Women disappeared, and depending on who they were, a massive search was either launched, or not. Some women were just more expendable than others. Always had been, always would be. I knew that, still my hand went instinctively to my neck, the choker around it. As a reminder, Gina had said when I asked her why she wore it. Out of understanding what happened to women like Teresa Marie once they went missing. To the memory of them. Maybe that's why she'd sent it to me. Out of responsibility, fear that if something happened to her, there might be no one left willing to remember Teresa Marie. I began to sense why George might not have seen the choker as an encouraging sign.

In the background, Polly's parrot squawked. I had heard somewhere that parrots only mimic one person. I hoped this one would spend the rest of its living days squawking "fucking half-cunt" at Polly, never giving her a moment's rest from Gina's memory.

"Well, I'll let you know if I hear anything," I lied to hasten my retreat.

"Oh yes, please do," she lied back. "You know where to find me."

"That's that," I said to Josie as I slammed the phone down. She flinched at the noise, or the anger behind it. I apologized, but the moment had passed. She continued the task she'd set for herself while I was on the phone: laying out bits of twine on the surface of the washer beside her, according to some pattern I couldn't decipher.

"Nothing left to do now but go back to Xandu's, I guess," I said. Josie didn't respond.

"I don't really see what other choice I have," I went on, as if Josie was trying to dissuade me, which she wasn't. She was completely absorbed in her task. Having set out twenty or so lines of string, she was starting the tedious process of tying them all together. A tangible task, finite, possibly useful. If she wanted, she could probably sell it to a junk shop, which was more than I could say about anything I'd done in the last forty-eight hours.

"Of course I could call the police," I said. Josie reacted to that with a slight jerk of her head. "At least report her missing." Although I realized Gina wasn't really missing. Not technically. Not in any way the police could afford to spend time on.

I picked a scraper out of the tool box and went to work on the piece of tar on the floor. It chipped off easily, leaving only a stain. Satisfied, I surveyed the laundromat, assessing what else needed doing. The mushroom patch caught my eye. I walked over, pressed around the rotting drywall until the sponginess under my fingers hardened into clean, solid wall. The damage was a bit worse than I had thought at first, but nothing I couldn't fix on my own. The idea of getting something done was heartening, surprisingly so. Embarrassingly so, considering what was going on around me. I was glad only Josie was there to witness my satisfaction.

As I went back behind the counter to get my tool box, Lois swept into the laundromat, up to the counter, and plunked down three dollars in change. "I'm not a con," she announced, and turned to leave.

I couldn't think of anything to say, but she turned back anyway. "I ran out on you without paying yesterday," she said. It looked like she might turn again, sweep back out the door, but then she shoved her hands into her pockets, shuffled a bit awkwardly and said, "I'm sorry." She was wearing a blue wool cap pulled down over her hair, covering it completely, a blue peajacket, jeans and running shoes. Had I passed her on the street I would have thought her a teenaged boy. A particularly miserable teenaged boy.

"Want some coffee?" I asked.

"No. Oh, OK," she said, still shuffling.

I poured her a cup. "You can have a seat," I said.

She didn't take one, remained standing by my counter gulping the coffee, shuffling.

"Is something wrong?" I asked finally.

"Uh uh," she said.

"More coffee?" I asked as she put down the empty cup.

"Uh uh. Thanks. It was good." She looked around the laundromat. "Nice place," she said.

"Thanks."

"Yours?"

"I manage it." Truth was, I was hoping to buy it, was slowly saving my money, making plans. I didn't tell Lois, though, was in no mood for her superior smile. I had a hunch the sort of risk-taking she admired didn't include trying to make a stand wherever it was life had happened to drop you.

A customer came in and needed change. I had to ask Lois to step away from the counter. She did, but as soon as I'd finished the transaction she stepped back. It didn't seem to occur to her that she might be disturbing me, keeping me from something I needed to do. I pulled out the tool chest, put the scraper back and pulled out the X-acto knife I would need to cut away the rotten wall.

"You know anyone around here who's hiring?" she asked. I wasn't sure I'd heard her right.

"Here, you mean? You'd like to work here?"

"Well, no. Not here." She looked away. "I was just thinking . . ."

"Did something happen at the bar?" I asked.

"No. Not really. I was just thinking maybe I would try something different for a while."

Why, I wondered. And why ask me? "I don't know anything offhand, but if you leave me your number I can ask around and get back to you."

She took the paper I gave her, but didn't write anything down.

"I don't give out my phone number," she said.

"So how am I supposed to get in touch with you?" I asked.

"I can check back in with you tomorrow."

Where did she get off, I wondered, asking me to find her a job, then thinking she could call the shots.

"What happened at Xandu's?" I asked.

"Nothing."

"So why are you looking for another job, then?" I asked.

She turned to leave.

I reminded myself that Lois wasn't just any sullen teenaged girl that I didn't like. She was one of the few living links between me and Gina that I had managed to find.

"Would you wait a second?" I called out. She turned back. "God, you're irritating," I said, which made her smile. I realized she hadn't smiled since she'd come in. "When would you want to start?

"It depends. I'm not sure." She was standing by my counter now, shifting from one foot to the other.

"How many hours a week are you thinking?"

She shrugged.

I still didn't like the way the conversation was going. Josie didn't seem to either. She was staring at Lois' back, her face twisted. Hostility, I guessed, but with Josie it was hard to be accurate about that sort of thing.

"I'll put out some feelers," I said finally.

She nodded but made no move to leave. I started rooting through my tool box again. Lois remained by my counter, shifting. I wondered if there was something specific on her mind she had wanted to unload when she first came in, or if it was just the same unspeakable anxiety I'd been feeling since Gina dropped out of reach.

"You're welcome to more coffee," I said as I walked back over to the rotting wall.

"Thanks," she said, but didn't take any. For the first time since I'd met her, she said goodbye before leaving.

"You're not hiring her" was Marlene's reaction, when she came in later that afternoon. Immediate, final, she didn't even pause to wonder what might have changed in Lois' mind, nerves or circumstances to bring her in to me asking about work. "This Lois is bad news."

"You don't even know her," I said, as if I did.

"I don't have to. She's a smarmy little addict who knows an easy mark when she sees one."

"For crissake, Marlene, she's—"

"She's laughing," Marlene cut in, pointing her finger at my chest for emphasis. "Let me assure you, this girl is laughing. She and Roger both."

"Roger has nothing to do with this."

Marlene ignored the interruption. "What did you offer her, evenings? Did you tell her she could just take the till home when she closed?"

"Oh shut up, Marlene, will you? I didn't even hint at hiring her."

"Yet."

"So what if I do? What's so terrible about offering a kid a second chance?"

"Nothing, if you don't mind being robbed blind."

"She's not going to rob me," I said, starting to collect my jacket and boots. The disappointment I felt was all the greyer for the stupid little hopes I had nursed all day. I had actually enjoyed Marlene's company the last few days, had dared to imagine we had turned some kind of corner, might become friends. "You of all people should be the last to stand in the way of a teenaged girl looking for a break," I said.

I shouldn't have, I realized. I'd struck a little lower than intended. Still, I was unprepared for her reaction. The sudden hardening of her face and eyes. The calm of her voice as it sliced me. Dead calm. "Don't you dare," she said. "Don't you ever."

I'd seen anger before, but this was something else again. The precision of it, the calm. *Hatred*, I would think later, when I could think. At the time all I could do was try to move out of its path. I sputtered an apology. Repeated it. "I'm really sorry," I said again. "I didn't mean . . ." I didn't know what I didn't mean. "I won't hire Lois if you don't want me to," I said, but it was over.

"I think this stuff with Gabe has me more worked up than I realized," Marlene said, her voice filling out from the flat edge it had been, her face released to an expression I recognized.

I wondered if I could have misread her, misunderstood. It had happened so quickly, no more than one flash of a blade, quickly retracted.

"I was overly touchy," she said, as if touchy was what I had just felt the edge of. "I'm sorry."

"I'm not going to hire anyone you don't want me to," I ventured.

She got up from behind the counter and began sweeping the floor. Short rough strokes. I knew her strokes, the way she held her hands low on the broom, the quick flick of her wrists in the corners. I had thought I knew her personality too, the way it flipped from bitch to Pollyanna and back to bitch again, never touching down between the two. I hadn't imagined what lay between.

"Oh, you fixed it," she said. She was standing by the wall I'd patched. "Nice work." She ran her hand over it.

I wondered if that was going to be it, a quick baring of teeth to back me off, then a return to how we'd always been. I had backed off, but the sweat on my back wasn't dry yet, my mind raced, my nerves were still on full alert. Slapped to a new awareness, I couldn't just slip back into where we'd been before. I wondered what lay behind what I'd just glimpsed. Anger? Rage? Fury? Hatred? I had already used those words up, wasted them on irritations and squabbles. I'd kept nothing in reserve, not guessing what was still out there calling to be named. Leave it alone, my instincts told me, but having seen it now, I couldn't.

"Something wrong?" she asked.

"No," I said. She looked at me expectantly. "I just want to make sure you're OK."

"Oh, you're sweet," she said, on automatic again.

"I'm sorry about what I said earlier," I said. She opened her mouth to speak, but I cut her off. "I didn't mean to throw anything in your face."

"It's OK," she said, giving new meaning to that expression. "I think I'm just a bit short-circuited tonight."

"You weren't when you came in." She had been in a good mood then. Her court hearing had gone well, better than expected. She had a peace bond her lawyer swore was enforceable, and a new, unlisted phone number. "Something set you off. Something about Lois. That whole situation," I added, inching as close to the subject of Roger as I dared. "You don't have to tell me," I offered, as though she was planning to.

She swept a bit of dust that had settled from the sanding I'd done earlier. Useless, I caught myself thinking. There would just be another layer for her to sweep within an hour or two. And a thicker layer waiting for me the next morning.

"You're not going to find Gina," Marlene said, after a while.

"What do you mean?"

"I understand why you want to hire Lois. What you're hoping will come of it and everything. And I don't blame you. I really don't, Tova. I might, too, in your place." She stopped sweeping for a second to meet my eye. "But you're not going to find her. You do know that, don't you?"

"No," I repeated, though it was true I was running out of ideas. Each path I had tried so far had dead-ended.

Marlene was sweeping again, clutching the broom. Like Lois, I thought, remembering Lois' routine on stage. Different rhythm— Lois' strokes were longer, smoother—but same purpose. The real work. Keeping things going. But what, I wondered, what was it, exactly, we were keeping going?

"Like it would be stupid to hire Lois if she's still working for Roger," Marlene was saying. "Do you know what I mean?"

I had missed most of what she'd said, but she was looking at me, expecting an answer.

"No," I said. "I don't know what you mean."

"Roger's dangerous, Tova."

"I know."

"You don't know," she countered, and I believed her. "I don't know what I have to do to get it through your head. He's dangerous, Tova. And so is Lois as long as she hasn't broken from him."

"Why did you say that about Gina?" I asked. "That I'm not going to find her."

Marlene shrugged. I didn't like how she was looking at me. Pity. Maybe disdain. "There's nothing you can do, Tova. Do you understand me? Nothing." I suddenly felt that was all I had been doing for years.

Gina had known, I thought as I walked west along Hastings. What I was doing with my life, or not doing. She'd made that clear enough.

It was after a girl had gone missing, the one after Teresa Marie. We were at George's. I was worrying about who was doing it, who might be next. Gina was eating. She was between fasts and was eating constantly. I asked her why she was eating so much.

"Because I'm hungry," she answered in a tone that could have ended the conversation. But then she asked, "Why? Do you think I'm getting fat?"

"No," I said. It was more the quantity of food going into her mouth that had caught my attention. It was a wonder more of it didn't end up on her frame. Most of it seemed to disappear inside her.

"I know I'm a fat pig," she said.

"What are you talking about? You are not. If anything you look better. You were too thin before."

"Tell Roger," she said.

"What do you mean?"

"I mean, call him up and tell him you like fat women. That you'll pay to watch a fat woman dance."

"I wouldn't—"

"That's true," she interrupted with a half-smile. "You prefer private shows. More informal. Free of charge."

"Oh please," I said. I didn't know why she had to keep milking that, why she couldn't let it go. *What's in it for you?* I wanted to ask.

"He told me last night he doesn't employ lard-asses."

"Roger? He called you a lard-ass?"

"Among other things."

"What an asshole," I said, as if this was a new discovery. "Maybe you'll get lucky and he'll fire you," I added. I even considered—out loud—the possibility that she was purposely putting on weight. Trying to get fired.

"*Trying* to get fired? Why would I try to get fired?"

"Why would you keep eating so much, given how he is? Maybe part of you is afraid you could be the next one to go missing."

"Ah, Dr. Freud."

"I'm not trying to psychoanalyze . . ."

"I'm not trying to get fired. If some psycho's got my number, he'll get me whether or not I'm working at the bar."

"Yes, but regular waitresses, saleswomen, cashiers—they're not the ones who are disappearing," I pointed out. *We're* not, is what I meant, and she caught it.

"That's a crock of shit, if I ever heard one. You think psychos never eat out in restaurants? Or that they don't go into stores? Or laundromats? None of you is safe—unless you think that since you're already half dead, no one would try to finish you off."

"I am not half dead . . ."

"Buried alive, then."

"I am not buried alive," I started to protest, then stopped. "Not all of us need to swing our tits in everyone's face to feel alive," I said.

I expected her to hit back. *You haven't seemed to mind. At least I'm willing to admit what it takes for me. To do what it takes. At least I am alive.*

"Anyway, I'm not trying to get myself fired," she said, suddenly flat. "I need that job. I'm good at that job."

"But it's not safe there now."

"You don't get to be safe until you're dead."

I turned up Gore to avoid the worst stretch of Hastings Street, and saw the man in the brown robe who'd been lurking around my laundromat . . . when? Friday. Could it have been only three days ago? He was sitting on the sidewalk, his robe spread around him like something that had spilled. I knew I shouldn't just walk past as if everything was OK. Everything wasn't OK. He wouldn't be sitting on the sidewalk in the drizzle if it was. But I couldn't approach him either, couldn't swallow my certainty that he was ready, waiting for the first fool to take the step that would place her within his range.

He's not dangerous, I told myself. What's dangerous is just walking by. What's dangerous is seeing a man spilled onto the sidewalk and telling yourself he's OK so you can get to wherever it is you think you're heading.

I saw a woman standing off the curb a few feet away. Dressed for work in her stilettos and fishnets, her face froze as I approached. The same expression as I'd seen on Marlene's just an hour before.

"Is that guy all right?" I asked, not taking another step toward her.

"Mind your own fucking business."

"I was just . . ." *Fuck you too*, I thought. "It's just, he looks like he might be sick. I was just . . ." Maybe she was right. So what if he was? What was I going to do about it? Take care of him? Or call the cops to have him carted off to some cell somewhere. Have her carted off too, for that matter. She wasn't looking all that OK herself. I probably wasn't either, if you got right down to it. I turned to leave, but she glanced over at him, then back at me and said he was all right. "He's not hurting anybody," she added.

I followed Pender to Burrard then turned south toward the

library. Things were a lot livelier at this end of town. Lots of suits, male and female, pouring out of office buildings, collecting at street corners waiting for lights to change. Crisp, well-wound, when the light changed they thronged across the street, then scattered to the families waiting for them at home.

The library was busy, a line of people waiting to check books out, and another, longer line waiting at the information counter. I took my place in it.

The woman behind the counter had a head of spiky curls that sprang out in every direction as if someone had surprised them that morning and they still hadn't recovered. When I showed her Gina's newspaper clippings she frowned.

"You don't know what dates these ran, do you?"

"Just the year."

She bent to read the clippings, pulling at a curl as she did so.

"Do you know what paper they were in?"

I shook my head.

She asked me to wait a few minutes. I'd been expecting that. It would probably be several lineups and a series of frowns before the final "I'm sorry we can't help you." I didn't expect that two minutes later she would flash a bright smile at me. Young, I thought, then decided it was the freshness of her expression. Unguarded optimism—I hadn't seen it in a while.

As she stepped out from behind the counter, she told me to come with her. She was wearing a short cotton print dress in blues and browns, crimson tights and combat boots. I followed her over to the microfilm department. "Start with this," she said, as she set me up with a box of film and showed me what to do. "I'll be at the information counter," she added. "If you need anything, come find me." *Anything*, she said. She could easily have limited her offer to *help*.

"Thanks," I said and felt my face relax into a smile.

The trial wasn't that hard to track down. It was in March and made the papers because of their ages. Marlene had been right about that. There had been more than one girl, several charges of rape and child procurement. He'd walked on all of them. The oldest girl was seventeen, the youngest thirteen. All were well known to the police.

The acquittal seemed to be due to lack of evidence, his death two years later a coincidence. He was only twenty-two when he died and, like Gina, well known to the police. There was no mention of any gang involvement, turf war, child prostitution ring, execution-style killing. He died in a fight outside a bar. Too much booze, a misunderstanding, a knife pulled. An undistinguished end to a sordid little life.

I turned off the machine, returned the films. It was 7:45. I had been at it two hours. Absorbed in my task, the tension in my muscles had eased somewhat. I could feel them tightening again, my mind beginning to race, dread resettling in me. I was tired, but couldn't face my empty apartment just yet; hungry, but didn't want to eat alone. I stopped by the information counter. The woman who had helped me was still there, talking to a colleague, laughing. I liked her laugh, too loud, unself-conscious. She could have a husband waiting for her at home, I realized, a batch of children, but I didn't think so. Just a hunch.

"Excuse me," I called out, too soft, but she heard, turned her open face to me. "Thanks a lot."

"Find what you need?" she asked.

"Yes. Thank you."

She smiled, then turned back to her colleague.

I walked down to the Hastings Street bus stop, then, still unwilling to face an empty evening in my apartment, kept walking down to the water. Cold and black, it lapped restlessly against the restraining wall. I thought of an ink drawing Gina had shown me once of a woman sitting at the edge of the water staring into a reflection of herself. The reflection was fragmented, her face a kaleidoscope of her features, unrecognizable except in bits and pieces. A horrible image, I thought.

"I did it last night," Gina said proudly.

"It's good," I answered, because it was. "A little disturbing."

"Disturbing?" She looked at it again, then grinned. "To me it's about opportunity."

Broken Water, she called it. I wondered now if she'd taken it with her.

As I followed the water's edge, I thought about the clippings, the ages of the girls involved. My mind flew to Lois, her shifting presence as she stood by my counter asking me about work. I knew she was scared, but of what? Something at the bar, I was sure, and wondered if that was what had scared Gina off. Although Gina had never seemed to want to get away from Xandu's. Even after Roger fired her, she had kept hoping he would take her back, and I was the one who had had to look for other work for her, scanning the classifieds, while she sat opposite me in the booth, distracted, her eyes flicking around the room.

"Dairy Queen's looking for someone," I said.

"I hope they find her," she answered.

"And lots of places are advertising for a receptionist. You could try that for a while."

"No I couldn't." She reached across the table to spear the last bit of cheesecake off my plate.

"How about being a waitress? Or a sales clerk at Club Monaco. Or here, a barrista."

"What's that?"

"You make espressos and cappuccinos. At Starbucks."

"Vomit," she said.

"Your attitude could use a bit of work."

"Nothing wrong with my attitude." She put down her fork and pulled her makeup bag from her purse. "Nothing wrong with refusing to bury myself before I'm good and dead."

I ignored the insult to me and scanned the page again. "You know, not that long ago most people in the world had to work as servants," I said. I had read that somewhere—I don't remember where.

"So what?" Gina asked. She was applying black liner around the edges of her lips.

"So things could be a lot worse than they are."

Gina's liner brush paused. She'd only done half her mouth. "Things *are* a lot worse than they could be, Tova." She completed the outline of her lips, smoothed out one edge where the liner had strayed, then picked up her pink lipstick. "You think you're not a servant?" she asked. "Just what do you think 'the service industry' means?"

"It doesn't mean servants," I said, wondering what it did mean, then. "I'm not a servant," I added. Angels, Gem had called us.

Gina finished her mouth. "What do you think?" she asked, pursing it.

"It's gross." Outlined like that, it stood out, swollen and pink, from her face.

"Does it look like a cunt?" she asked.

"Oh Christ, Gina. Can't you think of anything else?"

She looked in her mirror. "Maybe I should have gone for higher gloss." She fished in her bag for a pot of lip gloss.

A waste, is what I'd thought at the time. Of her energy, maybe even her life.

A waste, is what I thought now. My life. Cleaning up messes, basic maintenance, keeping things going. As if things were going so well they needed to be kept.

One of the angels, I heard Gem's voice as I cut up to Powell Street, but it sounded mocking now.

I stopped in at the Japanese Deli for tea. Hot, clear, light tea, I sipped it slowly, then realized how hungry I was. The couple at the next table were slurping huge bowls of steaming noodles. I ordered some for myself and had my face in the bowl with several noodles hanging out of my mouth when the woman from the library walked in.

She had pulled a leather jacket over her cotton dress and pushed her hair back with a headband so that now it stood straight up from the top of her head. Her face was more guarded than it had been in the library, but still optimistic as she scanned the crowded restaurant for an empty table. She looked a little odd standing in the doorway with her crimson legs, hopeful expression and upright hair. Oddly appealing. I smiled at her and motioned to the empty seat opposite mine.

"You don't mind?" she asked as she stood by the seat I had offered. "I won't bother you."

"You can bother me," I said and felt my face relax again.

"I'm Dara, by the way," she said as she sat down.

"Dara," I repeated. "Is that short for something?"

"Like what?"

We both smiled.

"I'm Tova," I said, extending my hand. Hers was smooth and cold from the weather.

I didn't mention that Tova means good.

An hour later, though, I was alone again. I'd enjoyed the break, enjoyed watching Dara's face as she talked, the glint in her eyes as she described the peculiar sorts of requests that people brought to her information counter, but ultimately, my mind had raced away from her.

"And what was it you were trying to track down, exactly?" she'd asked at one point. Renewed worry pulled me out of the comfortable conversation we'd been having, back to the clippings, to Gina, to the whole mess that I didn't understand.

I walked Dara to her bus, followed Pender east past Main, then turned back down to Hastings, toward Xandu's.

12

Pig Eyes was just inside the front door. I might have been able to brush by him, unbothered if not unnoticed, but I wasn't there to simply slip by. That much, at least, I knew. Beyond that I didn't have a plan.

"Don't you ever get a night off?" I asked him.

I thought that was reasonably neutral, but Pig Eyes was tense. Smart too, I sensed. Nothing I could put my finger on. Sharp, alert, nothing like the muscleheads I had imagined when Gina had talked about the guys she worked with.

"Lois working tonight?" I asked.

"She quit," he said.

"Since when?"

"Since you asked."

"Then you must be hiring." I don't know what possessed me.

I waited for him to respond. He looked away, his eyes on the opposite wall, his face wooden as he spoke. "Get out of here."

I should have. I should have slipped right back out the door onto Hastings Street before he had a chance to look at me again. Because when he did, it was with a coldness that clamped me shut.

"Get the fuck out of here," he said, and suddenly I couldn't.

I had experienced fear before that moment, but not the kind that pulls the breath out of your lungs and the will from your muscles. I was paralyzed for a second, and by the time he took his first step toward me, it was too late for any action on my part. He lifted me by my jacket, kicked open the front door and shoved me through it. Not hard, but hard enough for me to fall to the pavement.

I was more shocked than hurt. No one had ever lifted a hand against me before. I had imagined it, imagined how I might respond, not realizing I might not have time to respond. It had happened so quickly, was over so quickly. All I could do was sit on the sidewalk and tremble. I tried to stand, but my legs buckled. I sat some more and when I tried to stand again, managed, still trembling, to walk the few blocks over to George's. It wasn't until I was safely seated on one of his stools that I started to cry. Quietly at first, then loud gulping sobs as George, and probably everyone else in the place, looked on.

I felt George's hand on my shoulder and let him guide me to his office in the back. I sat where he placed me—on a cot by the wall.

"I'm OK," I said between sobs. To reassure George, maybe, or myself, that I *was* OK, that everything was OK, better than it might appear anyway.

"Wait here," George said, as if I was about to take off into the night. He returned with a steaming mug of tea.

"Drink some," he said.

I thought I couldn't, but as I held the mug tightly, raised it to my mouth and swallowed, the random jerking of my muscles calmed some. The tea was sweet, clear. I drank some more.

"What happened?" George asked.

"Nothing, really. It's just . . . everything," I said, wishing he was free to stay and coax the whole story from me. "Where's Helen tonight?" I asked. Helen usually worked with George in the evening, sometimes instead of him.

"Flu," he said, which, even in my chaos, I understood meant that George would be working eighteen-hour days until she could drag herself back in.

"I'm OK," I said. "Go back out front. I'll be out in a few minutes." He nodded and went back to work.

Alone, I sat on the edge of his cot, sipping my tea and crying. Not the breathless sobs that had overtaken me when I first came in. Wetter, deeper crying, the first since Gina had disappeared. When I finished the tea, I curled up on his cot, still crying. The hip I'd landed on hurt. I lay on it, concentrating on the dull rings of pain, the first physical companion I had to the emotional dread I'd felt all week. I felt my muscles release some of their tension; a heavy exhaustion flooded me, weighed me down. I knew I would sleep.

George woke me, his hand on my shoulder, his voice soft but as insistent as the light that forced itself under my heavy lids.

"Tova," he said.

I opened my eyes. They hurt. George was leaning over the cot, between me and the bare bulb of his desk lamp, but the light was still too bright. I closed my eyes. "What time is it?" I asked, wondering how I would be able to lift myself out of his bed to drag myself home to mine.

"Five forty-five," he said.

"You closing?" I asked and felt myself drifting.

"Opening." His voice brought me back.

Of course he was opening. In fifteen minutes. I opened my eyes again.

"Didn't you close last night?" Midnight was when he was supposed to close. Midnight until six the only hours the door was locked, no coffee on.

"I closed, and now I'm opening."

I wasn't the only one not ready to face the day. I could hear the exhaustion in George's voice. I forced myself to sit up, noticed there was no window in the room, just the cot, the desk with the lamp on it, a file cabinet, a closet, and two coats and a blanket on the floor. "Where did you sleep?" I asked.

"Where do you think?"

"You didn't sleep on the floor."

"The bed was taken."

I looked at him. He looked like hell, grey-faced and red around the eyes, but he'd shaved already, brushed his hair, dressed. I stood up. The room reeled, my hip hurt, and my spit turned sour in my mouth. I pulled the blankets taut on the bed, started tucking them in.

"It's all right. Leave it. Here," he said, handing me a washcloth.

I knew where the bathroom was, stumbled to it, held the hot wash cloth over my face, breathing in the steam, then placed it over my eyes. I rinsed my mouth out a few times, but couldn't sweeten it. When I came out, George had coffee on.

"I'm really sorry," I said to him. "You should have woken me. At least moved me onto the floor."

"What happened?" he asked, and I told him. About what I'd found out in the library, my stupid misadventure at Xandu's.

He didn't look surprised when I said I suspected Gina had worked the streets as a kid, didn't ask what I'd been trying to prove by going over to Xandu's. He listened wordlessly, without expression, doing his prep work while I talked. When I finished, he set a plate of scrambled eggs in front of me and went to unlock the door to open.

My stomach heaved at the sight of the eggs, but I took a bite of toast.

"Eat your eggs," George said, when he returned to the counter.

I did, as he finished his prep work in silence.

"Do you think she's OK?" I asked.

"She either is or she isn't. It doesn't much matter what I think about it."

"But what *do* you think?"

He stopped what he was doing and turned to face me. "I think I would feel a lot better about it if she hadn't sent you that choker."

"Why?"

"Think about it."

"What do you think I've been doing all week?"

He paused as if he was actually going to give some thought to my brain action over the course of the week, then shrugged. "It's just a gut feeling."

"Maybe she just took off somewhere to lay low for a while," I said.

"Maybe."

He didn't sound convinced. I wasn't either. The talk about her looking for Gem seemed more probable. It had come by me often enough to have the ring of truth to it.

"Some of the women at Xandu's are wondering what Gem's thing is about rescuing girls from Roger," I said.

"Gina told you that?" His face jerked, the first sign of life since he'd woken me that morning.

"Lois told me."

His features sagged again. "Lois doesn't know anything."

He looked old. I wondered how old, and felt ashamed that I'd never wondered before, never wondered where he lived, where he spent his time, who he was when he wasn't serving me pie and coffee. Gina had wondered, just like she'd wondered about me, making us both believe we were more than the drudgery that had become our lives. Or could be.

"She did work with Gina."

"Gina wouldn't tell her anything."

"Why not?"

He didn't answer.

"Do you think Lois is bad news?"

Out of my mouth, Marlene's words sounded stilted, false, but George didn't seem to notice.

"Not bad news, just desperate. Gina's not stupid enough to trust someone who's desperate."

"She's not stupid at all."

"She is if she's looking for Gem."

"Gem wouldn't hurt Gina," I said, sure of it, for no reason I could explain.

George raised his eyebrows, but didn't say anything. After a while he asked if I knew who the stiff in the dumpster was.

Of course I knew. The whole city knew. It was the pieces of women turning up in construction sites that no one seemed to know about.

"He was a lawyer," George said.

"I know that, George. I do read the papers." *A respected member of the criminal bar*, I had read out loud to Gina. She'd rolled her eyes.

"He specialized in pimps."

"Oh Christ, George, how would you know?"

"Gina told me."

"She did?"

"Yeah, she did."

"Yeah, well, she told me the Attorney General *is* a pimp."

George smiled. Sadly, fondly.

"She didn't mean for every single thing she said to be taken at face value."

"No, she didn't," George agreed, shaking his head.

"So what else did she say about him?"

"He was the lawyer who got her pimp off when she was living in Victoria."

"You mean . . . in the trial I just told you about?"

George nodded. "An airtight case, supposedly. She would never have testified against him otherwise."

"Gina told you that?"

George nodded. Once again he had stunned me.

"And it wasn't? Airtight?"

George shrugged. "Guess not. He got off."

"Who told her it was airtight, then?"

"The crown. They screwed up. *She* screwed up, actually—the prosecutor was a lady. She introduced evidence she wasn't supposed to. Or evidence she had gotten in a way she wasn't supposed to. I'm not sure how it went exactly. And two witnesses refused to testify at the last minute. The only adult witnesses."

"Why?"

George shrugged again. "Now, aren't you going to ask me who the prosecutor was?"

I waited.

"Jewel Ann Bonin," he said. The name registered, but it took me a moment to place it.

"Gem," I said just as he did.

"Gem," he repeated. "Gem was the prosecutor who screwed up."

"She's not even a lawyer."

"She was once. A Crown Attorney. And she screwed up. Royally."

I couldn't believe it. Wouldn't Gina have said something to me?

"It seems to me it shouldn't be that hard for a lawyer to figure out whether or not her evidence is going to get thrown out of court," George said. "There are rules about that sort of thing. You would think she would have troubled herself to learn them before she got a bunch of terrified kids up on the stand."

"How old were these kids?" I asked. Gina, I meant. He knew.

"Fifteen. Maybe sixteen by the time she actually testified."

"And Gina told you all this?"

He nodded. "And you know what gets me?" he asked. He didn't wait for my answer. "What gets me is how Gina talked about it. Like Gem did the best she could . . . like Gem was doing her some kind of personal favour. You know what I mean?"

I didn't. What I was thinking about at that moment was all those months of Gem hanging around the laundromat, the neighbourhood, and not a word from Gina. Not a flicker between them either. Not so much as a hint. Or maybe there was. I scanned my memory for something she might have said, a confidence overlooked, misread.

"So are you saying—"

"I'm not saying anything," George cut me off. "I just don't like that Gina may be off chasing after this Gem. She was bad news for Gina ten years ago. And from the sounds of things, she's worse news now."

The rumours, he meant. About Gem. The man in the dumpster.

"It doesn't sound like Gem was the one who was bad news for Gina ten years ago," I said.

George shook his head. "Now you sound like Gina. Gina thinks Gem was the one that got screwed over. *Maybe someone scared off the witnesses*, she said. *Right*, I said. *And then screwed up all her other evidence.*"

I couldn't answer, wasn't thinking straight. I needed to be alone to think. Away from George, at least.

"Like I said, there are rules about what kind of evidence you can introduce in court. A lawyer's supposed to know them."

"Gina doesn't need you to be mad at Gem for her," I said, one thing I was sure of.

"What do you know about what Gina needs?" George asked, the first time he had challenged me head on, rubbed my nose in the fact that she confided in him what she didn't even hint to me. I had no answer for him.

I tried to organize my mind while I walked to work, but I couldn't. I couldn't rise out of the hurt I felt that Gina had confided in George and not me, couldn't clear the confusion about the connections to Gina's life that were clicking into place all around me without adding up to any kind of whole I could understand.

I called the library as soon as I had Josie settled and the place ready for business. I had to know if what George had just told me was true.

Dara was in, and I asked her how I would go about finding the names of two lawyers involved in a trial ten years ago.

"This the same trial you were tracking last night?" she asked. I said that it was.

She thought for a minute. "You could start at the courthouse," she said. "Though, ten years . . . " She thought some more. "The Ministry, maybe."

"What Ministry?"

"The A.G. Attorney General," she said. "That's where I would start."

I thanked her, and there was a moment's silence between us. Then she asked me to call her back and let her know if I'd found what I needed. I suspected she didn't ask everyone who thronged her counter to call her back to follow up. Hoped she didn't, anyway. I told her I would.

Gina trusted me with those clippings, I thought as I dialled Marlene. That had to be why she left them for me. Because she did trust me. She trusted what I would do with that information. And the choker, too, I remembered as Marlene's phone rang. Gina trusted me with that, too. Me, and no one else.

"So let me try to get this straight," Marlene said when I finished telling her. "The pimp in the trial—he's dead, right?"

"Right," I said.

"And now his lawyer is dead too, right?"

"Right. But *now* is eight years later, don't forget. And ten years after the trial itself. We shouldn't jump to any conclusions."

"No one's jumping, Tova."

"What looks like a connection to that trial may just be a coincidence," I said.

"OK," Marlene agreed. "But the pimp and his lawyer *are* both dead now."

"That's right."

"And that customer of ours, Gem—she's being sought in connection with the murder of the defense lawyer. And now it turns out she was the prosecutor."

"Right."

"And one of the victims turns out to be Gina."

"Witnesses," I said. "I think Gina would be considered a witness."

"I don't know," Marlene said. "I'm getting a really bad feeling about all of this."

"Thanks, Marlene."

"But I'm sure Gina's OK," she added quickly. "Gina's a survivor."

I didn't push her on the hesitation in her tone.

The cops came by just after lunch. One cop. And I wouldn't have known it had I not recognized her from the days when she still wore a uniform and had come in to investigate a B & E. Detective Warren.

"I thought you always worked in pairs," I said.

"Just on TV."

I liked her smile, but not the blue eyeshadow she'd caked onto her eyelids. Someone had probably told her back in junior high that that was how to highlight her blue eyes, and she hadn't updated her look since.

"How have things been going around here?" she asked, glancing around the room. There were just two customers, both staring at their newspapers. Josie was gone, had started gathering her things together the minute the detective walked in the door. The smell, I assumed.

"Not bad," I said. It had been a year since anyone had broken in.

"Do you recognize her?" Detective Warren asked, flashing a picture of Gem. It was a good picture, her hair better cut than at any time I'd seen it, her eyes lively, her mouth not as tight.

"Yes," I allowed. "She's a customer."

Detective Warren looked at the picture again as if she might see something she had missed until now. "What do you know about her?"

"Not much," I said. That was true. "She bleaches her whites."

The detective met my smile then dropped it.

"What else?"

"Do you mind if I ask why you're asking?"

"Not at all," Detective Warren said, all servant of the people. "Did you know she's missing?"

"I've heard," I said.

"What have you heard?"

I couldn't believe I had looked forward to this interview just a few days before. A break in the routine, I had thought. Told Gina, no less.

"There are always rumours," I said.

"What kinds of rumours?"

I was starting to sweat now. I wiped my face and asked the detective if she wouldn't like a cup of coffee.

"No thanks," she said. "What kinds of rumours?"

"Oh, you know . . ."

If Detective Warren knew, she wasn't sharing the information with me. Her face was like wood now. Dead wood, I thought, my mind racing away.

"That Gem isn't her real name," I said.

Detective Warren nodded. Last time, she'd written things down. Which window was broken. What they'd taken. This time she wouldn't remove her eyes from my face.

"That's all, really. I hardly know her."

"When was the last time you saw her?"

"I'm not sure," I said. "Maybe a couple of weeks ago."

Detective Warren nodded again, then reached into her pocket to give me her card. "If you think of anything else—rumours, whatever—will you give me a call?"

I took her card. "Is that it?"

"You got something more you want to tell me?" She was smiling again, but not with her eyes. She'd been friendlier when she'd come in about the B & E. Easier going. Maybe I had been too.

I smiled back and shook my head. I expected her to thank me for my time, but she didn't.

"I want you to remember something," she said, looking me in the eye. "I'm on your side in this."

In what, I wondered after she left. I was sitting behind the counter, staring into space, numbly giving out change to the few customers who needed it. On my side in what, I wondered again and again. I was suddenly so tired I felt ill. I knew I couldn't call the Attorney

General's office that afternoon, didn't see how I would even find the energy to get on the bus home. I watched the rain drip down the front windows, the grey day darken. I heard the phone ring and reached for it. It was Lois.

"I haven't had a minute to ask about jobs for you, Lois," I snapped at her.

She was silent for a second, then said, "That isn't why I called."

"Sorry," I said. "I'm just . . ."

"I heard you came by the bar again last night."

"It's a free country," I countered. "Anyway, I heard you quit."

"Where did you hear that? I didn't quit. Who told you I quit?"

"The same sweetheart who told you I'd been by."

Silence.

"That's not really why I called," she said, her voice smaller than I had heard it yet.

I wasn't in the mood to play guessing games with Lois about why she had really called, and was about to tell her that when she said, "I think Gem's in Lethbridge."

"What?"

"I overhead two of the girls at work talking yesterday and one of them heard that Gem might have headed over toward Lethbridge."

"From whom? Where did she hear it from, Lois?"

"I don't know."

"Lethbridge." I tried to conjure up an image of the place but couldn't. "Why Lethbridge?"

"I don't know."

"Well, what did you overhear?"

"I already told you." Her voice was so small now, I was afraid it might disappear altogether.

"So these two girls were just sitting around chatting, and one happened to mention that Gem might be in Lethbridge?"

"Uh huh."

"And you have no idea why, or where they might have gotten that information?"

"Uh uh."

"Well, I don't know what to say."

Neither of us said anything.

"Well, thank you for telling me. Really. Thank you."

Lois was silent for a moment, then said, "I'm coming with you."

13

I didn't need a map to tell me where Lethbridge was. Far. Across several mountain ranges. A hard drive this time of year even if I had a car. Which I didn't. A night and a day on the bus, only to end up in an overlit bus station just as night was falling again, without the first clue which way to turn once I stepped out into the street. It might as well have been the moon.

"I didn't get a chance to follow up on that trial I was looking into," I said to Dara when I got her on the line. She was silent, letting the stupidity of my having called her hang between us. "I'm going to Lethbridge."

"Lethbridge?" she asked. "What on God's earth for?"

I found myself wondering briefly if Dara was religious, then heard her ask what I was going to do in Lethbridge.

"Find my friend," I said. I explained a bit about Gina, Gem, the call from Lois.

Dara was quiet again.

"How are you going to get there?" she asked after a while.

"Bus," I said, my mind filling with everything I had to arrange before I could get on the bus.

There was another uncomfortable silence between us.

"Well," she said, finally, "have a good trip."

"Lethbridge?" Marlene asked when she came on shift, looking at me blankly. "What's in Lethbridge?"

"I'm not sure," I admitted. "But if it's true that Gem was heading that way and that Gina was looking for her, then Gina could be there too."

"That's a lot of ifs," Marlene said flatly, starting to unbutton her coat. "Did it ever occur to you that maybe Lois is just looking for a ride out of town?"

It had, but ultimately it raised the same question: why Lethbridge?

"I'm taking the bus," I said.

"Lois doesn't know that."

She walked over to the closet. I thought if she took out the broom and started sweeping I might grab it out of her hands and hurl it through the window. She hung up her coat, then came behind the counter. A customer walked in. She smiled at him, then turned to me.

"Gina's not in Lethbridge," she said.

"She could be. She was looking for Gem."

"Gina's not looking for anyone. Gina's on the run. No one's going to find her now, and that includes you. Gina's a survivor," she reminded me. "If she's decided to disappear, she's gone." Marlene made the same slicing motion with her hand that Lois had when she compared Gina to a stray cat. I wondered if the mannerism was Roger's. "She's not about to let herself be found now."

Marlene looked at me, fondly, I thought, and shook her head. "I can't believe you're prepared to go chasing halfway across the country on something Lois told you."

"Lethbridge is hardly halfway across the country."

Marlene opened the till, then closed it again.

"If Lois really has heard something about Gem heading over to

Lethbridge, you know who else has heard, don't you?"

"I find it hard to believe that Roger's as all-knowing as you give him credit for."

Marlene shrugged. "His business depends on his keeping his ear to the ground. And like it or not, Roger is very good at what he does."

"OK, so maybe he's heard the same rumour I have. So what?"

Marlene shrugged again. She didn't seem to have anything more to add. I went over the day's totals with her, warned her about a washer that had gone during the afternoon, and said goodnight.

"You know, if you do decide you have to go to Lethbridge . . ." she said. I hesitated by the door. "You can borrow my car."

It wasn't just the offer of the car. It was the offer of understanding if, despite all reason, logic and common sense I decided I had to go. I started to cry again. She walked over to me by the door, touched my hand, and said, "I'm so sorry."

It wasn't until I was back at my apartment that I realized Marlene didn't have a car. I called her at the laundromat.

"Sure I do. The Festiva."

I remembered it but hadn't seen it in months. I'd assumed she'd sold it.

"It's at my mother's. I didn't feel safe carting the kids around in it, you know, with Gabe following me and everything. He knows the car." She hesitated. "But maybe now, with my peace bond . . ."

It seemed like an awful lot of weight to be putting on one piece of paper. I'd seen her peace bond. It wasn't that impressive. Light-weight paper, a few signatures. But I couldn't turn down Marlene's offer now. What had felt like the purest generosity had shifted into a test. Was I willing to take her car, or was I too afraid to enter into her life even that much? Had I marked her as someone to feel badly for, but to keep as separate and clear from as possible? I asked her where to pick up the car. She gave me her mother's address.

"What about the laundromat?" I asked. "I won't be more than a few days, but I guess . . ."

"I'll do your shifts," she said.

"You can't. What about your kids?"

"I can manage for a few days," she said. "Who knows? Maybe Lois will show up asking for a job." Her tone was almost light, teasing.

"Lois will probably be coming with me."

"Oh Jesus."

"Steve or Diane can probably fill in a shift or two," I said. The owners; it had been a few years since I'd had to ask them to fill in. It was that long since I'd taken more than a day off.

"Don't even think about the laundromat. It'll be fine," Marlene said, taking away the one thing in my life I felt some pride in.

I was surprised how much there was to arrange before I felt free to leave. At another time I might have found it reassuring. Andre said he would water my plants. I showed him around, explaining their needs. "Always worrying," he said. "You leave me to worry about the plants. You worry about having a good time."

"I'm not going for a good time," I said. I hadn't told him where I was going, and he hadn't asked.

"So worry about having a bad time. Just don't worry about your plants."

I paid my bills, cleaned up my apartment, emptied the refrigerator. All that was left was picking up the car and Lois, and telling George. It seemed important to tell him, not to simply disappear.

The phone rang as I was about to leave. Dara.

"I was just thinking," she started, awkwardly. "If you still need the names of those lawyers, I could probably find that out for you pretty easily."

"You could?" I didn't ask her why she would want to.

"Yeah, I could."

"Well, thanks," I said, then asked her how she got my phone number.

"That's what I do," she said. "Track things down. Not that you're a thing," she added hastily. "But really, if you think it might help . . ."

"It would be a big help."

There was a moment's silence, but not uncomfortable this time.

"What time's your bus?" she asked.

"I'm driving," I said and told her about Marlene's offer.

"You ever driven to Lethbridge this time of year before?" she asked, her voice dubious.

"No. Not at any time of year."

"Well, I have. Don't mess with the southern route. It can be awful. Take the Coquihalla."

"I'm coming with you," George said as soon as I told him where I was going.

"You can't."

"Why not?"

He walked over to the door, flipped the sign from *Open* to *Closed* and walked back to me. "Give me an hour-and-a-half to empty the place out and make a few arrangements," he said.

"Maybe I want to go on my own," I said.

"On your own with Lois, you mean?"

"No," I said and realized I actually felt relieved about George wanting to come. It helped me believe the trip might be worth taking. "But this is my trip, George. I don't want to stop to sleep anywhere. Or to eat. And I don't want music blaring in the car. Or conversation."

"Who said I wanted to talk to you?" he asked.

"And I'm not waiting an hour-and-a-half to leave. I'm going to pick up the car—"

"We can take my car," he interrupted.

"I'm going to pick up the car," I continued, "and then if you're not ready, I'm leaving anyway."

"Cut the crap," he said. There was something about the way he said it. Serious, intimate almost. So I did.

"I haven't even told Lois we're going yet," I said.

I thought George might roll his eyes, make some comment about leaving Lois behind, but he'd also cut his usual crap. "You get the car," he said. "I'll make my arrangements here, and we'll drop by the bar on our way out of town."

"I can't go into Xandu's," I said.

"I can."

"What if she's not there?"

"She will be," he said.

Marlene's mother was expecting me. "Tova?" she greeted me through the crack of the door. I said I was and she unhooked the chain lock. I could have been anyone, could have snapped the flimsy chain with one hard push. I didn't point it out. She looked worried enough as it was. She was thin, painfully thin, her hair drained of whatever colour it had once been, her face deeply lined. Worry, or too many cigarettes. Maybe too much of both.

"Come in," she said.

I didn't want to. I sensed she wanted to talk, to worry with me over Marlene, the children. To speculate about Gabe. I just wanted to take the keys and be gone.

"Coffee?" she asked.

"No thanks." The place reeked of cigarettes and old coffee. The light in the hall we'd moved into had turned Marlene's mother yellow. She was yellow, I realized. Sick with something that had eaten her flesh and turned her yellow. Hepatitis, I thought. Or worse. Marlene hadn't mentioned anything.

"Marlene speaks so highly of you," she said.

"And of you," I said. She smiled, her teeth too huge for what was left of her face. "I don't think she would have gotten through this past year without you," I added. A clumsy gift, which she promptly rejected.

"She would have found a way."

And will, filled up the awkward silence between us.

"So the car's around the corner on Cotton," she said, handing me the keys.

"On the street?" I said. I don't know what I was expecting. A guarded garage maybe.

She nodded and we thanked each other in unison.

I was nervous walking to the car. I looked around me before unlocking it, checked the minuscule back seat, my heart thumping. This was Marlene's life, I realized. And not even. I could at least fall back on the comfort that if Gabe recognized me he would leave me alone.

I drove over to Clark, then down to Hastings, watching my rearview mirror. I didn't think I was being followed, but wondered if I would know it if I was. Had watching her back become second nature for Marlene? It was convenient to think that it had, comforting, but I suspected it didn't really work that way. That fear remained fear. That more of it didn't make you better at it, but simply wore you out faster, eating away more and more of your life in ever-bigger bites.

When I got back to George's, he was almost ready to go.

"Make yourself useful," he said, handing me two duffel bags.

"What am I supposed to do with these?" I asked.

"I'll let you figure it out," he said and ducked back into his office. It occurred to me that his office was where he lived. His home.

I went outside and started cramming George's bags into the trunk. "You can't bring anything else," I said when George came outside with one more bag.

"You'll thank me for it later," he said. He deposited the bag on the floor of the passenger's side then wedged himself into the seat.

"What are you going to say to the creep at the door?" I asked as we drove over to Xandu's.

"As little as possible," he answered. Terse for George. I wondered if he was nervous.

I pulled up to the curb half a block away from Xandu's. "I don't want Pig Eyes to notice me," I said.

"I won't be long," he promised.

Fifteen minutes later he still wasn't back. I hadn't even left town yet and already I had run into a problem I didn't think I could solve on my own. I couldn't go after George, unless I wanted Pig Eyes to follow through on what he had started with me the night before. And I couldn't just drive off. All I could do was continue to wait, but for how long?

Ten more minutes passed. I decided to set a limit. Fifteen more minutes. If he wasn't out by then I would leave. He would know where I was. Assuming he was OK, that he had passed as just another customer, that Lois hadn't given anything away to anyone she shouldn't have, that Lois was what she appeared: a girl scared into vacancy. It was a lot to assume. Fifteen minutes, and then . . . I couldn't imagine what I might do, but I didn't have to try for very long because five minutes later George reemerged. Lois was right behind him.

"Sorry it took so long," he said getting into the car.

"I had to get changed," Lois added as she crawled into the back seat.

A half-hour seemed a long time to get changed, but I didn't pursue it. It was almost midnight, and my mind was on Gina. I continued east along Hastings, and turned onto Highway One East with George beside me and Lois' vacant face in my rearview mirror.

The exits rolled by. Burnaby, Port Coquitlam. We crossed over the Fraser River into Surrey. No one spoke. "Did you bring any of your stuff with you?" I asked Lois.

She wiped her face, and I saw, as we passed under a light, that she was crying.

"I have some cash."

"Whose?" George asked.

"How much?" I asked.

"I've been saving up."

"Whose?" George asked again.

"What difference does it make?" I asked him.

"I just want to know who's coming after us. Besides Gabe, that is."

"Who's Gabe?" Lois asked.

"It doesn't matter," I said. "Is the cash yours?"

"Most of it. Roger's not going to come after me for five hundred dollars anyway."

"You took five hundred dollars from him?"

"He always has small change hanging around."

I still thought of small change as quarters and loons. "Is that what took you so long? Jesus, Lois. He'll kill you when you get back," I said.

"I'm not going back."

I felt a small lift inside myself. Despite my confusion and growing sense of dread about what was happening around me, I heard Lois' words and felt a lift inside myself, an opening of possibility. Not the kind of possibility I had once felt watching Gina, but possibility, nonetheless.

I drove quickly through Langley, past Abbotsford, but Chilliwack was still thirty kilometres away when I realized I was going to fall asleep.

"Who's taking care of your place while you're away?" I asked George. His eyes were closed. He didn't answer.

I glanced in the rearview mirror. Lois' face was turned to the window. I couldn't tell if she was sleeping or staring into the passing darkness.

"Hello?"

"I thought you didn't want conversation," George said, his eyes still closed.

"I need coffee, conversation or loud music," I said.

I glanced at George again and saw him smiling. He reached into the pack he had at his feet and pulled out a thermos. "I have coffee and tea," he said. "What will it be?"

"Coffee."

"Coffee," Lois said from the back.

He pulled out three mugs and started pouring. Just the smell of the coffee picked me up.

"Helen's running the place," he said, handing a mug back to Lois.

"I thought she had the flu."

"She got over it."

"Can she run it without you?"

He looked at me, crookedly. "Of course she can. Her daughters are going to help her," he added.

"I didn't know Helen had kids. How old are they?"

"Teenagers. Fourteen and seventeen, I think. Nice girls."

"Can their mother pull them out of school just like that?" Lois asked.

George turned around in his seat. "I think they'll probably work after school."

"Oh."

George turned back and Lois pressed her nose back against her window.

"My mother never let me miss school," she said after a while.

George met my glance. "Where is your mother?" he asked, his tone light, artificial-sounding.

"Pocatello."

"Idaho," I added.

"Thank you, Miss Tova," George said to me. "Does your mother know where you are?" he asked Lois.

Lois didn't answer.

"Don't you think she's worried about you?"

"If she was that worried about me, she could come find me. I've sent her a few postcards. It couldn't be that hard to find me if a person were looking."

Sixteen, I thought.

"I can drive," George offered as we approached the first Chilliwack exit.

"It's all right," I said, and it was. Everything felt oddly all right. Removed from the grey grid of East Vancouver's streets, my life inflated with possibilities, expanded to fill the unlimited space around me. I felt an odd sensation, power possibly, as each exit approached then receded. Each one seemed another barrier to Gina that I had taken us past. I pressed on the gas, the needle fluttered to 110 kph, then 115. At 120, the car started to rattle. I eased off, no less powerful, as I nailed the last Chilliwack exit.

"More coffee?" George offered. I held out my mug. "You should fill the tank in Hope," he said.

"It's still half full."

"Top it up anyway. You won't find any stations for a while."

A large sign flashed up ahead. *Highway One Eastbound. Snow and icy conditions. Drive with caution.*

The next sign flashed the same warning about Highway Three. The next one about Highway Five. For the moment it was still only drizzling.

"Is the Coquihalla Number Five?" I asked, though the sign had just said it was. My confidence dipped slightly as I realized I'd forgotten to bring a map.

"Number Five," George said. "It's a bitch in snow."

"Dara said it's the best way to go."

"Who's Dara?"

"A woman I met at the library."

I tensed, waiting for the inevitable: *You been holding out on me?* But George too had been released from his grid. "Yeah, well, I don't know how much driving she does, but the truckers avoid it like the plague in snow. Too steep." He raised his hand until it was perpendicular to his wrist, in case, in our peculiar new circumstances, I'd forgotten the usual meaning of the word steep.

"We'll decide in Hope," I said.

"I hate Hope," Lois contributed.

"As a state of mind?" George asked.

Clever, I thought, but Lois appeared to have missed his wit.

"I got stuck there on my way to Kamloops once. It was hardly snowing at all but the fucking driver refused to go. Just sat on his ass having smokes."

"Watch your language," George said.

"What were you doing in Kamloops?" I asked, my short-lived confidence abandoning me completely as something I couldn't identify nudged at me.

"Visiting a friend," Lois answered vaguely.

I remembered the picture Gem had showed me. A girl, younger than Lois, missing. From Kamloops.

"The only way out of Hope is straight up," George was explaining to Lois. "Used to be, the only way was the Fraser Canyon. People arrived there alive and thought God had delivered them personally. That's why they called it Hope."

"That true?" I asked. Lois was staring out her window again.

"True enough," he said. "Even now, it's a hard drive."

I had driven it once, in summer. Kept my eye on the road as it wound through a break in the steep dark walls that enclosed Hope. Further on, it was hot and dry, the sides of the canyon falling to the river below, Lynn's head resting on my shoulder. Nothing had seemed easier.

"Should have called it Hopeless," Lois muttered to her window.

14

It made no sense to take the Coquihalla. That much was clear as I pored over the map I had bought at the gas station in Hope. Lethbridge was due east. The Coquihalla cut north before providing an outlet to the east. "Yeah, but look why," Lois said, tracing her finger along the twists and turns of my chosen southern route.

"Mountains are a fact of life in B.C.," I reminded her, not about to turn aside, even temporarily, for the sake of a straighter-looking line. How bad could it be, I asked myself and pressed on.

As we climbed out of Hope, drizzle changed to rain, rain to sleet, sleet to snow. We entered a quieter, muffled world. If it only stays like this, I thought, then wondered, if *what* stays like this? I focused on the weather. Snow might be falling, but it wasn't hurling itself against the car. The road was blanketed in white, but the tires were still turning, rolling us forward. We might be moving slowly, but we were moving.

Toward what?

I concentrated on the road, the wheel in my tight grip. We reached what I hoped was the summit, only to round another bend and climb some more. I glanced at my watch: 2:30, and I was beginning to feel the hour. With every inch we climbed, the snow thickened. Trees heavy with snow waved and bowed along the sides of the road. Like sentries, I thought, marking our passage.

Exhaustion smothered the confidence I'd felt earlier; horrible possibilities I'd kept at bay all day flooded my mind; the coffee that had propelled me to Hope collected in my bladder. I pulled off to the side of the road at the Allison Pass summit.

George jerked awake. "What's the matter?" he asked.

"Nothing. I have to pee."

The cold air was bracing after the closeness of the car. I breathed deeply as I walked away from the car, smelling nothing but clean cold, hearing nothing but the blood rushing in my own head. Snow collected on the arms of my jacket, my shoulders, my hair.

I heard a car door open, slam, George's muttering, then his strong stream of pee. I dreaded him walking toward me, roughing up the perfect new surface of snow, his voice, too loud, prodding me back into the car. He walked around to the driver's side, opened the door and got in. I crouched for a while longer, watching the snow collect on my arms, then stretched again, filled my lungs with cleansing air and folded myself into the passenger's seat beside George.

I closed my eyes, felt us coast, then, after a while, turn into the sharp slow switchbacks down to Princeton. When George stopped the car, I couldn't tell if I had been awake or asleep. It had stopped snowing. The trees by the side of the road were gone, the darkness around us empty. "Where are we?" I asked.

"Outside Osoyoos. I'm just going to take a leak."

The next time, he jarred me out of deeper sleep. I couldn't bring myself to open my eyes. I heard him fill the car, but was asleep before we pulled back onto the highway.

I didn't feel the car stop after that, just became aware, gradually, of the absence of motion. My right arm and right foot were both numb. I shifted, opened my eyes. We were in heavy forest again, at the edge of a lake encircled by dark hills. George was sitting beside me staring out the window.

"Where are we?" I asked.

"Christina Lake."

The day was as bright as it was going to get. Grey.

"I thought it was supposed to be sunny in the Interior," I said.

"And B.C. is the Hawaii of Canada," George answered. His tone was grim.

Too long a night, I thought, sorry I hadn't relieved him at the wheel sooner. It was morning. I had slept long, if not comfortably. My own mood had improved, was verging on hopeful. We'd come further than I'd expected, would be in Lethbridge sometime within the next twelve hours.

Lois stirred in the back. "Where are we?" she asked.

"Hawaii," I told her. She smiled sleepily and tried to stretch. She was built small, but not small enough. I got out of the car, flipped my seat forward and released her.

It felt good to stand. I felt my blood start to move again, my foot and arm tingle then burn as they came back to feeling. I walked over to the lake. Inky black, it lapped at the ice forming around its edges. It would be a bleak place even on a sunny day, I imagined, the trees absorbing any light the mountains allowed to filter in. *B.C.'s all right if you like trees*, I remembered Gina saying once. I didn't. They were too dark, too brooding, and crowded too close around me. I felt desperate to break into the open.

I walked back to the car. George was still sitting in his seat. He had the window rolled down and was smoking a cigarette.

"Aren't you getting out?" I asked.

I knew he had a stash of sandwiches in one of the bags he had packed. Maybe even a pie. That would be just like him, to bring along a pie.

"We have a problem," he said.

My first thought was the car. Maybe it had died, coasted into this spot. A problem, but nothing we couldn't handle. Still hopeful, I remembered the vacuum I'd left in Vancouver. My life. It was probably still sucking blindly, wondering where I'd escaped to, hoping to pull me back in. Next to that, a dead car seemed easy.

George handed me a newspaper. That day's *Province*. Confused, I asked where he got it.

"Grand Forks. I filled up there earlier," he said just as I saw the headline.

My body took in the words before my mind could. My stomach tightened, then heaved. The words seeped in—*former Crown Attorney, suspicious circumstances, Jewel Ann Bonin.*

She had been a prosecutor, then a social worker. She was somebody's daughter, somebody's sister. They were taking her back to Toronto for burial. Family members weren't sure why she was in Lethbridge. Her work took her all over Canada, her father said in a statement to the press. Police were investigating, but had no comment at this time. Anyone with information was asked to come forward.

I stared at the article, reread it. The trial wasn't mentioned. Maybe the police hadn't noticed the link between two of the homicides they were investigating. Maybe they had, but hadn't leaked it to the press yet. I wondered why Detective Warren hadn't told me she was dead. Had she had to wait for the family to be notified, or had she been playing some kind of cop game with me? *I'm on your side in this,* she had said as she left, knowing I would hear what *this* was soon enough.

The boundaries of the parking lot were marked by rocks. I sat on one. I knew I had to think, but couldn't. I could only feel my heart smashing against my chest, could only see Gem's face, her high smooth forehead, her unblinking eyes. The article hadn't said how she had died.

George got out of the car and sat down beside me. Neither of us spoke. When Lois came I handed her the newspaper. She read it and handed it back to me.

"Gina didn't do it," she said.

I couldn't respond, and George didn't seem to want to.

"You got a smoke?" Lois asked him and he handed her his package of cigarettes. She sat down on the other side of me and lit up.

"No one said Gina did it," I said, fury and disgust taking me over. "Why would you even think it?" And when she didn't answer, "What's wrong with you?"

"What's wrong with *me*? What's wrong with *you*?" she asked and stomped off in the direction of the lake.

George and I stayed where we were, neither of us speaking.

"The little bitch took my cigarettes," George said after a while.

Our eyes met for the first time since he'd shown me the paper.

"Should we leave her here?" I asked.

"She's just a scared, stupid kid," he said, and I felt ashamed.

I found Lois standing by the lake, her arms wrapped around herself.

"It's freezing here," she said when I stood beside her.

"Let's go," I said and we walked back to the car.

"I'm starving," she announced as she climbed into the back seat. George pulled a sandwich out of his bag and handed it to her.

Egg, it smelled like. I opened my window and took a deep breath, then pulled back onto the highway heading east. No one asked where we were going.

"They're going to try to pin it on Gina, you know," Lois said, filling the car with egg breath. Her face and voice were so expressionless I wanted to smack her. Just for a reaction, I told myself, and concentrated on breathing.

"Why would they?" George asked.

"Because everyone knows that the guy in the dumpster is the lawyer that got her rapist off. And that Gem's the one who let him. And everyone knew Gina was looking for Gem."

Everyone, I heard Lois say, and wondered why I had been the last to find out. "Gem didn't *let* him," I said.

"Still," Lois said, and I realized she was probably right. Of course the police would have noticed the link. Detective Warren was probably checking into it right now. Running Gina's entire life through some computer. "Lois has a point," I said to George. "Gina will probably be a suspect."

"I doubt the cops even know Gina exists," George said.

"George has a point," I said to Lois.

"I'm still starving," Lois said. "You got any more sandwiches?"

"You're not really hungry," George said. Gently, I thought.

We drove in silence for a while, climbing again. The trees were heavy with fresh snow, the sky heavy with more to come.

"Gem was strange, you know," Lois said.

"No, she wasn't," I answered. She was friendly, friendlier than most. She noticed me, noticed what I did, and called me an angel.

"I'm not saying she deserved what she got, but she *was* sniffing around for months before she disappeared. Some of us thought she was a cop at first—we thought you could be one too," she said to me. "But just at first. Even Roger asked about you."

Lois waited. Perhaps I was supposed to be honoured that Roger had asked about me.

"So Gem kept coming by with pictures of different girls who'd gone missing," Lois went on. "For months. Like every missing kid in the province came to Roger straight from the bus station and he snuffed them or something. Jesus."

"What do you mean?" I asked.

"I mean, all those girls—they could be anywhere. Roger may

have a few underaged girls working for him, but that doesn't mean . . . Gem was strange. She told Gina the whole justice system was one big pimp service. And that's the only reason—"

"Gem was crazy," George cut Lois off.

"And that's the only reason what?" I prompted Lois, but George cut us both off.

"It doesn't matter what she thought. She was crazy."

"But I want to hear what Gem told Gina anyway," I said. If we were going to look for Gina, it seemed like we should at least know what she thought she was chasing, or running from.

"That's all," Lois said, as if George had reminded her of a cardinal rule she had momentarily forgotten. "That's all I know," she chanted.

"What did Gem mean by a pimp service?"

"Think about it," George said. "She loses big in court, so she decides it can't possibly be something she did wrong. It must be a rotten judge. A rotten system. An entire justice system devoted to ensuring that pricks like that walk. Makes a lot of sense, if you're crazy."

He had heard it before, I realized. He'd had time to react in private, think it through and dismiss it as too crazy to believe.

"Why are you so furious at her?" I asked. His anger felt off, wrong. Especially now.

"If she dragged Gina into something . . ." His voice trailed off.

"Like what?" I asked.

"Anything."

I tried to think what to ask next. It was hard. My mind felt like someone had poured something sticky into it. Sticky and grey. Everything looked grey, felt grey. I tried to focus on what Lois had just said, but I was losing it, losing Lois and George, losing everything but the grey air around us, the dark trees lining the road,

191

trapping us on the grey pavement that was leading us . . . I had no idea where.

We drove on in silence, past Trail, and Salmo. George lit another cigarette. I opened my window wider.

"It's freezing back here," Lois said.

"I'm sorry, but if I close my window I'll puke all over George."

"Do you want to pull over?" George asked.

"I want you to stop smoking."

George inhaled deeply, then put out his cigarette.

"Gina didn't tell me all that stuff, exactly," Lois said from the back.

"All what stuff?" I asked.

"See, Gina never really let on to me that it was Gem who told her about the courts being rigged and everything. I didn't even know Gem was a lawyer. I thought she was just a social worker. It was only after she split, and all the rumours about her and that guy in the dumpster started—I forget who I actually heard it from, about her being a lawyer."

Roger, I thought. I don't know why. It was my first thought, and once it popped into my head I couldn't chase it out. Roger let it slip that Gem had been a lawyer. And not just any lawyer. The lawyer who'd lost her big case to the prick that had just turned up dead.

"So once I knew Gem was a lawyer and that Gina was a whole lot tighter with her than she'd let on—"

"Gina pretended she didn't know her, right?" I cut in.

"No. She knew her, all right. You couldn't help but know her. She was always buzzing around the place."

Like some kind of flea, I could hear Gina saying. I could see her face as she said it and felt a wave of longing so intense it felt like nausea.

"But I thought Gina couldn't stand her," Lois continued. "She used to tell me social work was for people whose lives were so dead they had to go poking their noses into everyone else's just to try to suck off a bit of a thrill."

Longing turned to shame, but my nausea remained.

"So it came as a bit of a surprise when I saw them together at a coffee shop once. All the way over at Granville and 63rd. I'd gotten dropped off there and went in to get some change for the bus, and there they were. At a table right by the back. Like two lovebirds, heads together, talking—like Gina really couldn't stand this woman, right?"

"Did they see you?" George asked.

"Naah. They were too busy with each other. But that's when I began to put a few things together."

She was ahead of me there. "Like what?" I asked.

"Well, just that there were things Gina wasn't letting on about."

Not that far ahead of me.

"Did you tell anyone?" George asked. "That you'd seen them together?"

It was George who was ahead. Thinking, anyway.

Lois hesitated, then said, "No."

"It's OK if you told someone, Lois," George said. "Why wouldn't you? I mean, here's some social worker poking around, Gina pretending she wants nothing to do with her, then you see them hanging around together some place where they obviously think no one will ever see them—why wouldn't you tell someone?"

"I didn't tell Roger."

"I didn't mean Roger. But one of the other girls at work? Why would you keep it a secret?"

"Because Gina was my friend."

I was only a close friend of hers, I remembered Lois saying, one muscle in her jaw rippling her still face. *Why would I know anything Gina was up to?*

I looked in my mirror to see Lois staring blankly ahead.

"Roger knew anyway," she said. "I didn't tell him anything, but he knew anyway."

Like it or not, Roger is very good at what he does, I heard Marlene telling me.

"He called me over to the bar one night when I was working the floor, poured me a Coke—on him, he said—and asked if I knew why he'd fired Gina. I thought at first he was trying to tell me I was getting too fat—I'd put on a few pounds—but then he said Gina had been holding out on him, and that's why . . ."

"Holding out on him?"

"He said Gina and Gem had some kind of game going and that's why he'd fired her. You know, that he couldn't have people working for him who were playing mind games like that."

"Did he say what kind of mind game?"

"Uh uh. And I was too scared . . . see, I thought he must have figured out that I had seen them together and I was holding out on him."

"Oh, come on, Lois. How could he have figured out what you had seen? It's not like you carry him around in your back pocket. There's no way . . ." I said. Unless she had told one of the other girls at work.

I glanced at George. He looked straight ahead.

I pulled into a gas station near Creston and asked George to fill up. He raised his eyebrows. "I need to make a call."

The phone was outside. I wanted to call Marlene. I wasn't sure why—a fresh perspective, a reminder of a life that just hours ago I had wanted to leave behind. I dialled the laundromat and reversed the charges. Marlene answered on the second ring.

"Where are you?" she asked.

"Gem's dead."

"I know. I saw the paper." She paused. "You have to come home now, Tova."

"I'm going to Lethbridge," I said.

"What for?"

"To find Gina."

A truck roared past, drowning out Marlene's response.

"What?" I asked.

"Gina's not in Lethbridge," she said.

"She could be. She was looking for Gem."

"She may have been looking for Gem at one point," Marlene conceded. "But once she hears about this . . ." She paused. "Gina's a survivor," Marlene pronounced yet again, as if she hadn't already delivered that particular piece of wisdom to me. "Gina isn't going to run toward something like this. You should come home now, Tova. You're not going to help Gina by being stupid."

"I'm not being stupid," I told Marlene, and went back to the car. George was washing the windows. Lois was curled up in the back seat eating an Aero bar. She tossed the wrapper out the window. I picked it up and tossed it back onto her seat.

"I'm heading back to Vancouver," I said, as I got into the car. "Gina's not in Lethbridge," I explained, though no one was arguing. "Even if she was looking for Gem, she'd have run miles away by now. She's not an idiot."

"I'm not going back to Vancouver," Lois said.

"Then I'll drop you off in Creston. It's right at the Idaho border. You can catch a bus from there down to Pocatello. Be home in time for dinner. Breakfast at the latest."

"I'm not going home," she said.

"Vancouver or Pocatello," I said. "Your choice."

"You can drop me in Kamloops."

"We're not going anywhere near Kamloops."

"Well, I'm not going to Vancouver, and I'm not going home."

"The party's over, Lois," George said.

"This hasn't been about partying," she said, her voice even flatter than usual.

"What is it about, then?" I asked.

She didn't answer.

"No one runs away without a reason," I said. "You must have had a reason."

"I had a reason."

"And?"

"And it's none of your business," she said.

Fair enough, I thought. "But aren't you tired of being scared all the time?" I asked.

"I'm not scared all the time," she said. "And anyway, there's worse things than being scared."

I thought about that. "Like what?" I asked.

"Like having to clean the kitchen floor and the bathroom floor with a toothbrush. Both floors. Every inch of them. With my father standing over me to make sure I didn't miss anything."

"Are you serious?" I asked, but could see from her face in my mirror that she was.

"What happened if you missed a spot?" George asked.

"Then I had to lick it."

"The spot you missed?" I asked.

"Everything."

"Rogers Pass is a killer," George said as we stared at the map. If he caught the coincidence in his phrasing, he didn't let on. "We'd be better to backtrack to Osoyoos, then cut up to Kamloops through the Okanagan."

"I don't want to backtrack," I said.

"You'd rather just circle in on it?"

"What's in Kamloops?" I finally thought to ask Lois.

"I was there once," she said. "I have a friend there," she added.

"Don't you think you should go back to the States?" I tried again. "I don't mean Pocatello. But just over the line. If it were me—"

"It isn't," she cut me off.

Fair enough, I thought again as I started for Rogers Pass.

We spent the next few hours in silence. George passed around sandwiches at one point. Lois sat unmoving, her forehead pressed against the windows. The weather had cleared. The scenery was beautiful. Clear sky, the open country I'd been craving just hours before.

We turned north at Cranbrook, west at Golden. George took over the wheel. It was dark again, but the moon was almost full. "Pretty night," I said, just to see if I could still talk about something normal.

"We'll be lucky if the weather holds in the pass," George said.

Lucky is not what I was feeling, but the weather did hold.

15

George waited until Lois was asleep. It was late by then, and we were well into our wide useless arc. George said Lois' name, softly at first, then louder. When she didn't answer, he asked what I made of what she had told us.

"About Gina and Gem?"

"Yeah."

"I'm not sure," I said. I had been thinking about it through the afternoon and evening. All during the long drive up the valley from Cranbrook, I'd been trying to push beyond my exhaustion, fear, nausea and confusion, trying to make sense of what was happening around me. Had been happening for quite a while, it seemed. "I don't understand," I admitted to George. "I mean, if Gina and Gem wanted to get together, so what? So they knew each other ten years ago. Why all the secrecy?"

George didn't answer.

"Why the little drama about a secret rendezvous at a coffee shop in the middle of nowhere?" I went on, anger gaining the edge on understanding.

"Granville and 63rd isn't the middle of nowhere," George said quietly.

"Depends how you define somewhere," I muttered. Lynn and I had driven through that neighbourhood a few times when we'd first moved to Vancouver. Big houses, big trees, empty streets—

it had been years since I'd been anywhere near that part of town.

"Gina couldn't afford having Roger find out," George said. "He runs a tight ship, Roger does. Doesn't brook any interference."

"I'm not confused about why she kept it from Roger," I said. "What I'm wondering is why she kept it from me."

"She kept it from everyone."

"Not from you." I heard the slight whine in my voice.

"From me too, Tova. I knew about the trial. I knew she was looking for Gem when she took off." For a photo, she'd told George. And he'd believed her. "But I didn't know they'd been hanging around together in between. Having coffee. Whatever the hell they were doing."

"You really didn't?"

"Not until Lois told us."

I glanced at him to see if he was also hurt by Gina's omission, but couldn't tell.

"Don't you wonder why she'd have kept it from you?" I asked.

"Of course I wonder." He looked my way for a second. "You're not the only one who's been wondering about it." He looked back at the road and said, "I guess she figured it wasn't any of my business."

"And that's it? That's enough of an explanation for you?"

"It's going to have to be, isn't it?"

I glanced at him again but still couldn't read his face.

"What happened with you and Gina?" I asked.

"What do you mean?"

"I mean, what was between you?" I asked.

"Nothing," he said, then smiled at the pavement straight ahead of him. "There was nothing between us. At least none of the shit she usually put between herself and everyone else. I still believe that." He thought for a moment. "She was different when we were alone. It's hard to explain. Quiet."

I couldn't imagine Gina quiet, tried to remember if I had ever seen her mouth still, but couldn't.

"So what happened?"

"It's not like you think."

I didn't know what I thought.

"There was a long time when all we did was lie together. Every night. That's all we did. Lie together." He glanced at me again and flashed an embarrassed grin. "Pretty hot, eh?"

"Not everything's about sex," I said.

He nodded, the grin gone. "I don't think she knew that before." He shrugged. "She started talking again after a while."

I imagined them lying together, side by side, skin joined, perfectly still. I'd never seen her still.

"And when she started talking again, it was different."

Different how, I wanted to know. "What did she talk about?"

He shrugged. "What she talked about didn't matter. Sometimes it was about something that had happened at work, or something she'd seen on the street. Sometimes it was about herself, her past, whatever, but not usually. Usually it was just this or that. She'd come over, lie with me, and start talking. I can't really explain what it was." He looked at me again to see if maybe I understood without his having to explain. I didn't. "I would find I was holding my breath, you know? She'd be talking about some dress she saw in a window that she thought might look good on her, and I'd be holding my breath. Or something that Lois had said that upset her, and I'd be holding my breath. Strange, but then I realized what it was."

"What was it?"

"She was telling me the truth."

I didn't answer. I thought about all the conversations I'd had with Gina, and wondered if she had ever told me the truth. She might have. I thought hard. I didn't know if I would recognize it. George had. It had made him hold his breath.

"I didn't know Gina," I said after a while. "Not really," I added, although George wasn't raising any arguments.

"You knew her," he said quietly. "You can never know all of someone."

"She didn't let me," I said.

George didn't answer.

"She might have if I hadn't been so . . . I was like one of her customers."

"No, you weren't."

"I was, George. You don't know." A voyeur, she called me. "You don't know," I said again. "There were times she might have dropped her act, but I never really let her. I never asked her anything. Not really. Not about herself. Never picked up on anything."

"So what? I didn't either," he said. "I just lay there."

And held your breath, I thought. "I didn't even do that."

"Don't torture yourself," he said.

"I'm not," I said. "I'm being honest. Now I'm the one who's telling the truth. I was like a parasite with her. I was like this half-dead creature who attached myself to her because she seemed fully alive. All I did was try to suck some of her energy into myself. Some of her life."

He didn't argue, but I didn't think he was holding his breath.

"Gina liked you," George said. I noticed we were talking in the past tense. "And she trusted you. She may not have told you things, but that doesn't mean she didn't trust you." He looked at me. "Not everything is about talking, you know."

I nodded.

"She wouldn't have let you suck her life, as you put it, if she didn't trust you with it."

I knew that. "But what was she trusting me with?" I wondered out loud.

George didn't answer.

"Being OK," I said. "Commonplace." The painstakingly boring drudgery of being OK, day after day, year after year. The tediousness of it. The comfort.

George reached over to take my hand in his, squeezed it for a second, then released it.

We stopped in Salmon Arm for gas. Lois stirred in the back, but didn't get up. Back on the highway, the headlights of oncoming trucks were beginning to confuse me. Irritate me.

"Aren't you getting tired?" I asked George. He was still driving.

"Kamloops is just over an hour away. Maybe a little more."

I closed my eyes, but the shaking of the car when trucks passed was just as irritating as staring into headlights.

"So what did you make of Gem?" I asked George.

"Not much," he said, no longer in the mood to talk.

"Is that why you helped spread the rumour about her?"

He shrugged, refusing to bite.

Another set of headlights appeared in our path. I closed my eyes until the car stopped shaking.

"Did you really believe it?" I asked. *Do* you believe it, I wondered. "You know, that Gem could have been the one who—"

"What does it matter now?" George cut me off. "Gem's dead. Gina's missing. Who the hell cares what I thought then? Who the hell even remembers?"

Gem is dead. Gina's missing. For one second I grasped the reality of what that meant.

"I'm worried," I said and thought what an inadequate word worried was. Stupid. Worse than useless. "I'm really worried about

202

Gina now," I tried, then suddenly felt trapped. By George, by the close air of the car. By my brain that couldn't even find the words to catch what raced around inside it. My heart started racing. I opened the window and breathed in deeply a few times. My stomach cramped and I realized my body too was giving out on me. It would explode rather than hold the anxiety inside it for one minute longer.

"Would you mind stopping the car?" I asked. He did, and I got out. I didn't know where we were, but the air was sweet. I noticed that as my stomach cramped and heaved. I moved away from the car and crouched in the darkness. My bowels emptied, and I felt ashamed. Even in the dark, with no one to see me, I felt ashamed as I soured what had been sweet just an instant before.

"You all right?" George asked when I got back into the car.

"We need to speak to the police," I said. I tried to think how the police might help, but couldn't right then. "Because Gem is dead," I tried. My voice sounded thick. Slow. "Gem is dead," I said again. "And if Gina is going to be found alive now, I think she needs someone on her side besides us."

I'm on your side in this was what Detective Warren had said. Not in everything. But in this. I clung to it.

"We were OK for her for a while," I said. *OK*, I thought. That's what we were, all we were. Trapped in OK. "But whatever it is that's going on, Gina needs more than a couple of . . . losers who can't think of anything more useful to do than drive themselves in circles wondering what's going on."

George didn't answer right away. He looked straight ahead in the darkness.

"I'm not a loser," he said after a while.

"The point is . . ."

"The point is, I'm not a loser." He waited a moment. "I'm just not a winner this time around. The going's rougher when you're not a winner."

"I know that."

"No, you don't. No one does. No one even thinks about it."

"I do," I said.

He shook his head as if I had disagreed with him. "It takes more guts," he said. "A lot more guts."

"What if you don't have enough?" I asked. "Guts."

George shrugged. "I don't know," he said. "You go crazy, I guess."

I thought about that too. Whether craziness was just a shortage of the guts necessary to face your life. I didn't think so.

"Do you really think Gem was crazy?"

He shrugged again. "I'm no shrink."

"I know, but do you think there could be anything to what she said to Gina about the courts? Or do you think she was just crazy?"

He thought about it. "Every house has a few rotten boards," he said. "It doesn't mean the whole thing's going to cave in. That's what makes you crazy. Waiting for it to all cave in." He thought some more. "And being crazy, I guess, is thinking it already has."

Better to keep washing the clothes, cooking the food, brewing the coffee, is what I thought he was getting at. Keep on keeping it going as if it hasn't all caved in. Like Nero, I supposed. Only he was an emperor. Like Nero's servants. Somehow, I wasn't with George on this one.

"What about Gina?" I asked. "Do you think she was crazy?"

"She was doing what she had to."

"You mean taking off her clothes every day for a roomful of men?"

"Taking her clothes off for food and rent," he corrected me, anger creeping into his voice. "For food and rent and the clothes she got to put back on." I noticed he hadn't answered if he thought she was crazy. "Because she wasn't ready to just throw up her hands and say this is all for shit."

Not crazy. In his book, at least. But the way things were looking, it was all for shit. Had been for Gina anyway.

We decided to sleep as soon as we reached Kamloops. Nothing seemed urgent except that, the need to stretch out on a bed and sleep. We pulled off the highway and into the first motel we saw.

"I only have one room left. Two beds," the owner said, peering past me and George into the car to see how many people we were trying to sneak by him.

"Two beds is fine," George said.

I assumed they would turn out the sign that flashed "Vacancy." They didn't. They gave us a room right beside it. I knew it would seep into my sleep and turn my dreams against me. We pulled the curtains but our room pulsed anyway.

"We won't notice it once we shut our eyes," George said, but I knew I would.

I curled under the covers and shut my eyes, but I couldn't shut anything out. I took it all in: the throbbing neon, the roughness of the sheets against my skin, the creak of the bed as I breathed, the easy rhythm of Lois' breathing beside me, the nagging sense that it was all for shit.

I remembered my mother's voice. Not her face. It had been years since I could remember her face. But her voice. It was soon after she left us, when she still called from time to time. "Try to be like a reed," she told me. "People are happiest if they can be like reeds."

"What did she mean?" I asked my father.

"Flexible," he said. She must have told him the same thing. "Flexible in need. Flexible in want. Flexible in expectation," he throbbed. Then he gathered all the photos we had of her, snipped them into pieces and burned them in a bonfire on the back porch. Flexible I couldn't be. It was her I kept wanting. But reed-like, I had planted myself in the child I was when she left. I watched the bullrushes by the sides of rivers and lakes. They bowed and swayed with the current, but didn't move. I didn't move either, was afraid to, in case happiness came back and no longer knew where to find me. But she never came back. It was all for shit.

Sunlight woke me. I dreamed it was a flashlight aimed at my eyes. I opened them expecting to be blinded. The room was bright, sunlight pouring through the space around the curtains. George was still sleeping, but Lois' side of the bed was empty.

I took a long shower and when I came out, George was awake.

"Sleep well?" I asked him.

"Where's Lois?" he asked.

"I don't know."

"I want to get going."

I said I wanted to go look for Lois and would meet him back at the motel coffee shop. I found her by the river. She was sitting on the pebbly beach, by the foot of a pier.

"I think there's otters or something diving out there," she said, pointing to a large V-shaped ripple a few feet from shore.

"Otters are extinct," I said. I don't know why. Irritation, maybe, that she would run off like that. And that I'd run after her.

"They're not extinct," Lois said. "Sea otters were almost extinct once, when people hunted them for their fur. But they're coming back now. And river otters were never extinct. I saw a show about it once."

"I'm sorry I said they're extinct," I said.

Another V formed off shore.

"I dreamed about a river last night," I said. "I don't remember much," I went on, though she hadn't expressed any interest. "Mostly that I was a bullrush."

"You dreamed you were a bullrush?" she asked, looking at me for the first time.

"In a marsh. Stuck in a marsh."

"I don't know whether that's cool or sick."

"Me neither," I said.

She looked back at the river. "I'm staying in Kamloops, you know."

It was a statement, but she lifted her voice at the end of it. Just a bit.

"What's in Kamloops?" I asked again.

"I told you. I like it. I had a nice time here once."

"She still here, your friend?"

Lois shrugged.

"What's your real name, Lois?" I asked her.

She turned to me. "Star," she said. "My real name is Star. Lois is just my stage name." She looked back at the water.

"Why don't you come back to Vancouver with us?" I asked.

"I can't."

"Why not?"

"You know why."

"You can give the money back to Roger."

"You don't know anything."

"Maybe not, but what are you going to do here?"

Out on the water something dove. Her otter, maybe.

"At least it's not raining here," she said.

The sky was a pale, cloudless blue.

"It's probably not raining in Vancouver today either."

She threw a pebble into the water. It made a circular ripple before it sank.

"What are you going to do here?" I asked again, although I knew. She hadn't even finished high school. Even if she had, she wasn't a legal immigrant. What could she do?

"Start over," she said.

"You're too young to start over. You haven't even started once yet."

"You don't know anything," she said again.

"I know there are people and things you have to run away from. Like Roger. Your father. You were smart to get away from them."

A slight smile as she asked, "You think so?"

"Yeah, I do. But you've run enough now. As long as you're still running, you haven't really started anything." I stopped to think if that was really true. I had stayed perfectly still for years and not started anything either. Not much, anyway. "You have to stop running at some point and start something," I concluded, just because she seemed to be listening.

"Like what?"

"It doesn't matter. Whatever you decide is worth starting. That's for you to figure out."

"Like working in a shithole laundromat for the rest of my life?" she asked.

"It's not for everyone," I conceded.

We went back to the coffee shop. George wasn't there yet.

"What if he left without you?" Lois asked.

"He wouldn't," I said. "Not everyone does that kind of thing, you know."

We ordered coffee and waited for George.

"No one leaves Roger," Lois said to me.

"He tell you that?"

She nodded.

"People leave him," I said, remembering the scar on Marlene's chest. If he touched Lois I would kill him, I decided. Right then and there, I made a decision. A promise to myself. If any more harm came to Lois by way of Roger, I would take a knife and plunge it into his white pulsing neck.

"Cream and sugar?" the waitress asked.

"Please," we said in unison.

Lois measured out her sugar, carefully. One even teaspoon. She stirred her coffee, then measured one even teaspoon of cream.

"I knew that guy who was killed, you know. The lawyer." She was still stirring her coffee. Slowly. Carefully. "He used to come to these . . . these shows we had. These private shows."

"What private shows?" I asked.

"Roger arranges these . . . shows sometimes. Nothing weird. It's just private. For customers who don't want to be seen at Xandu's for some reason."

"Like what kind of reason?"

"Oh, you know, their jobs, that kind of thing. No. *Positions*. That was the word they always use. *Position*." She met my eye with a wry look, almost a smile, then her mouth twitched down. "Like that's suppose to impress us."

George showed up at that moment, a Vancouver newspaper in hand. "I don't know why they call this thing a newspaper," he said. "It's so packed with bullshit about the tax revolt there's no room for any news."

"What tax revolt?" Lois asked.

"Haven't you been following it?" George asked. "There's a

revolution on. Property owners over on the West Side are tired of having to pay their taxes."

"That's what happened in America," Lois said. Wistfully, I thought.

"This isn't America," George said. "No one's saying anything about life or liberty."

"Happiness," Lois added.

"Pursuit of happiness," he corrected, but it didn't seem to make an impression on Lois. "This isn't America," he said again, leafing through the back pages for any news that might have something to do with us.

"Lois was just telling me about these private shows Roger puts on sometimes. For customers who might not want to be seen in some place like Xandu's."

"Private shows?" George asked. He looked up from the paper. "What kind of private shows?"

"Nothing weird," Lois said again. "Just private."

"What do you mean, 'private'? Where does he have them?"

"At customers' houses."

"And you did some of those shows?" I asked.

"Uh huh. We all did."

"Gina?" George asked. I had the feeling we had just moved into territory he hadn't heard about yet.

"By the time I started working, Gina was already working the bar mostly. She was getting too . . ."

Too what, I wondered. Too fat? Too old? Too mouthy? Lois didn't fill it in.

"So you were telling me how they try to impress you. The customers," I said.

"Oh yeah, you know how men like that . . ."

"No. No, I don't."

Lois sighed. Overwhelmed, I supposed, by the task of explaining the habits of important men to a nothing like me.

"So who are these pricks?" George cut in. "Doctors? Politicians?"

"Judges."

"Judges," George repeated. He was surprised. I could hear it in his tone. Very surprised. But you would have to know him to catch it.

"Not just. Lawyers too. A few doctors now and then."

"But judges," George said.

"So what?" I asked.

"What do you mean, so what?" George asked, incredulous at my naiveté, I assumed. Although not as incredulous as I was at his.

"So what if judges also frequent the occasional peep-show?"

"It's not just a peep-show," Lois said. "I mean, usually it is. But sometimes—"

"Just girls?" George interrupted, disappointing me. It was the "just" part. As if Lois' "yes" might edge it all toward OK.

"Depends on the night," Lois said.

"And all underaged, right?"

"Mostly."

"Mostly or all?" I asked.

"I don't know. It's not like anyone runs around asking us for our ID cards. What does it matter?"

"It matters, Lois. You know damn well why it matters."

"Now you sound like Gem," she said, not entirely nastily.

"So this guy who was just murdered," I said. "The lawyer."

Lois nodded.

"He was a . . . customer . . . at these private shows?"

"Yeah. He was."

The waitress came to take George's order.

"Coffee," he said. "Black."

"I didn't really know him. You know, personally. I wasn't his type."

I glanced at George. He was nodding. The waitress brought his coffee. He forgot to thank her.

"He liked Native girls," Lois said, and glanced at me.

She was waiting for me to say something. I didn't know what. She didn't go on.

"Teresa Marie?" I asked.

She nodded. "He liked Terry," she said.

I looked at George again. He was still nodding. Almost hypnotically. "Did any of you talk to the police?" George asked. "After Terry disappeared?"

"Uh uh. I was going to, but Gina told me not to. That's when she told me about the courts being rigged and everything. I told her I wouldn't. I promised her I wouldn't. Talk to the cops."

But Gem was dead now, Gina missing.

"We're going to have to now, I'm afraid," I said, and realized I was. Very afraid.

We paid for our breakfast, and Lois said she guessed she would come back to Vancouver with us after all. "Might as well," she said. "What am I going to do here?"

I was glad she didn't want to be left alone. It seemed like some kind of start, though of what, exactly, I couldn't say.

16

"*Might as well* take the Trans-Canada," George said. "Save the toll."

"Might as well," I agreed. It would add an hour to the trip, but I was in no hurry to get back to Vancouver.

George drove. We didn't speak. I began to notice a funny smell in the car. Fishy. Rotten. Fear, I thought, sniffing the air around me, until I realized it was my shoes. They'd gotten wet on the beach.

"That's quite the river," George said at one point. I looked out my window at the Thompson.

"Do you think Roger killed her?" I asked.

"She's not dead," George said.

"I mean Gem. Do you think Roger killed Gem?"

"Not personally."

"But you think it's possible he might have had something to do with it."

"It's possible."

He runs a tight ship, I remembered George saying the night before. *Doesn't brook any interference.*

"Who wants to see where the Thompson meets the Fraser?" George asked a while later.

Nobody did, but he pulled off the road at Lytton anyway. "To get gas," he said. "But since we're here . . ."

I had seen it once already. With Lynn. I'd been thrilled by the way the two rivers travelled side by side without mixing, the ribbon of blue alongside the wider brown Fraser, until a bit downstream, they came together into one muddy churning current. At the time, I had seen it as an omen about the future of my relationship with Lynn—a good omen. I was wrong. Lynn hadn't wanted to be swallowed by mud. I imagined her now, clear and liquid, miles upstream.

I called Detective Warren from Hope. She wasn't in, but when I said what it was about the operator offered me another officer. "I'll wait for Officer Warren," I said. She told me to call back in half an hour.

"Can't you wait until we get home?" George asked.

I'd been wrong about the weather. The sky had been so pale coming down the canyon that I hadn't noticed the blue dulling to grey. At Hope it was impossible to miss. A light-eating sky, the mountains looked flat against it. Lifeless.

George noticed too. "Another front moving in," he commented. Soon the grey would darken and lower itself, obliterating the tops of the mountains altogether. *Like living inside a coffin*, Gina had once described the coast. Until then I had imagined coffins as red satin.

I asked George to find a pay phone in Abbotsford. He pulled off the highway and into a pink and peach mall. That's all there seemed to be in Abbotsford. Pink and peach. Sunbaked colours, I thought, momentarily reassured that I wasn't all that was monstrously out of place. I dialled the police station.

"I tried to call you back," Detective Warren said before I even started talking. "Where are you?"

I told her I had heard about Gem.

"Yes," she said flatly. "We're investigating it as a homicide."

Suspicious circumstances, the newspaper had said. Of course it was a homicide.

"A friend of mine is missing," I said. "She knew Gem."

She asked me how Gina had known Gem, when Gina had disappeared. When I said Gina had worked at Xandu's she asked me to come into the station.

"Why?" I asked.

"I would rather talk to you in person."

"Why?" I asked again, sinking. "You haven't heard something about Gina, have you?"

"No," she said, "but from what you've just told me . . ." She hesitated. "I'm extremely concerned about your friend."

I don't know if it was the tone in her voice or the fact that she called Gina my friend—I told her I would.

"They're going to try to pin it all on Gina now," Lois said when I got back to the car. Her voice was high, pinched, as if her supply of air had suddenly been cut off.

"Pin what on Gina?" I asked, though I thought I knew where she was heading.

We were still parked by the pay phone. A car honked behind us. We were blocking the laneway. George started the car, drove us out of the parking lot and back onto the highway.

"Everything," Lois said. Then: "Maybe she did help Gem."

"Shut up, Lois," George said, not unkindly.

I watched Lois in the rearview mirror. She seemed about to speak, then didn't.

"Help Gem with what, Lois?" I asked.

Lois was quiet for a bit, then said, "Gina used to make fun of you, you know."

I suppose that some part of me had been waiting for this.

"She would imitate you, the both of yous."

"You," George corrected. I wondered if he had wanted to be a teacher once. Or a parent. Way back when he still wanted on a regular basis.

"The way you sit around clucking your tongues like a couple of old hens. *Oh, did another girl go under? What a shame. Tsk tsk.* Couple of losers."

Losers or old hens? I wondered. There was a difference.

"She wasn't like you. She wasn't about to just sit by and watch what was happening."

"What did she do, Lois?" George asked.

Lois didn't answer.

He should have asked me, I thought. I knew what Gina did each time another girl went under. She swore. And sometimes she wore an article of the missing girl's clothing.

"What are you saying?" George asked again. "What did she do?"

"Something besides clucking."

George lit a cigarette and passed the pack back to her.

We drove on in silence for a while, the two of them smoking, me trying to breathe.

"You really think she could have done it, Lois?" George asked after a while. "You really think either of them could have killed that prick?"

"That wasn't what I . . . " She fell silent again. "If they thought he had something to do with killing Terry, then yeah, maybe they could have."

"Well, you're wrong," he said. "And even if they had, what came of it? Gem's dead. Gina's missing. Running for her life."

Or worse, I thought.

"There are no avenging angels," George said to Lois. "That's something you might as well get through your head right now. If you're waiting for some kind of angel . . ."

Marlene was also into angels, I found myself thinking, she had even lent me a book about them. There was a whole section on how to recognize your own guardian angel. Among all the others, I guessed.

"There's just the cops and the courts," George went on. "And the few people who are decent enough to cluck when another girl goes under."

Wrong, I thought, Roger's neck pulsing white in my mind.

We drove through Langley in silence, and I remembered the surge of feeling I'd had as we flew through it in the other direction. Power, I'd thought at the time.

Something that had been nagging at me all week finally formed into a question.

"What did Gem do with the kids she found?" I asked Lois. "I assume she did find some . . ." I turned around. Lois nodded. "It's not like she could send them home to live happily ever after. And there aren't exactly a million jobs out there waiting for kids who decide to . . . There aren't a million jobs, period."

"Any," George said softly beside me.

Lois didn't answer. We drove over the Fraser River. On the other side, a blot of stucco housing was spreading up the mountainside like an out-of-control infection.

"I always had a bad feeling about her," George muttered beside me.

"Gem?" I asked.

He nodded. "From the minute she started hanging around. I wasn't sure what it was, but people like her, people who are on some kind of personal mission . . ."

I waited.

"Who think they've been personally anointed to fix the world . . ."

But she *was* anointed, I thought. We all are. *Tikkun Olam*, I found myself remembering. That was the Hebrew word for it. Repairing the world. We were all personally anointed. Obligated, really. In every action performed, no matter how humble, the opportunity was there. With every pie crust we rolled, every shirt we folded, every hello we exchanged with another person, we were obligated to find our own way to make repairs.

"Life isn't fair," George was saying. "Never has been. Never will be. And if you don't find a way to live with that . . ."

"Maybe she did," I said. "Find her way."

We crossed into Coquitlam's strip of megastores. It started to rain.

"There are safe houses," Lois said from the back. Her voice was so quiet I wasn't sure I had heard right.

"Safe houses?" I asked.

"If you wanted to get out, she wouldn't turn you in to your parents or the cops. I don't know about jobs, but you could go—"

"Where are they?" George interrupted.

"I don't know. Nobody knows. We just know they're there."

"But what good are they . . . how would you get to one if you didn't know . . . ?"

"You got word to Gem. She would take you."

"And how did you get word to Gem?" I asked.

"She wasn't hard to find," Lois said.

No one spoke for a while. We passed into Burnaby. It was drizzling now.

"Is that what she was doing in Lethbridge?" George asked. "Trying to get to a safe house?" I didn't know if he was referring to Gina or Gem.

Lois didn't answer.

"Was one of the safe houses in Lethbridge?"

"I have no idea," Lois said. "If anyone found out where they were, they wouldn't be safe anymore."

I looked at George. He was stroking his phantom beard.

"Are you going to tell the police about this?" he asked Lois.

"I'm not going to tell the police about anything."

"So what are you going to do now?" I asked.

"I don't know yet. Not work in some shithole laundromat for the rest of my life."

"I mean right now. George and I are going to the police station."

"Well, you can just drop me off right here, then. I'm not going to talk to some pig about Gina."

We dropped her off near her apartment at First and Commercial. When she paused before closing the car door, I told her to drop in at the laundromat later. She said she would, but I wondered if that was the last I would ever see of her.

Detective Warren looked different. Her face, mostly. It seemed to have stiffened and gone pasty under the streaks of rouge. The face of a dead person, I couldn't help thinking, and wondered if that was it—another of the dead in drag as the living. I wondered how many of us there were.

"Are you all right?" she asked and waited. I couldn't answer. We were squeezed into an office so small and stuffy all I could think of was how long it would be before we had breathed up whatever air there was. Maybe we already had. I inhaled shallowly, but all I took in was the smell that had filled me in the car. Failure, I thought now, but it smelled more like dead fish. I looked down at my shoes, dry, but still putrid with trout or salmon, or maybe just bits of algae out of their element. I glanced at Detective Warren's shoes. Dead, but odourless. Strips of dead cow buffed to a high black shine. Like the choker around my neck, I remembered, touching it, wishing I could take it off, hold it between my fingers, and bring it up to my face to inhale.

"Would you like a glass of water?" Detective Warren asked. I nodded. She still might be on my side, but I couldn't tell anymore.

"I won't quit until I get to the bottom of this," she said at one point, and I saw her at the bottom of Vancouver harbour, weighed down with whatever it was they attached to bodies they didn't want surfacing. I wondered if the smell escaped anyway, no matter how weighed down the body. Or the life. If the secret escaped and infused the clear blue water with its rot, and that's what we smelled as we walked the beach thinking about fish and algae and nature taking herself back. I wondered if that was what I would smell for the rest of my life as I lay in my bath after work each night, the rot of all the women who'd sunk before me pouring out my faucet (*Just a bit of runoff in the reservoir*, city officials assuring me still).

"Why did you tell me they were investigating Gem's death as a homicide?" I asked the detective.

"What do you mean?"

"What else would you be investigating it as?"

She hesitated before answering. "A suicide." Detective Warren hesitated again, then told me Gem was shot in the head. "Once. Through the mouth."

"And you thought suicide?" I said.

"I wasn't involved in the investigation at that point, but yes. There were only her fingerprints on the gun."

Lack of evidence again, I thought. Gem's ultimate downfall. The catch-all whitewash for all of our lives. Then I wondered why Detective Warren was telling me this.

"There was no sign of struggle," she added.

If a woman with her brains blown out of her head wasn't a sign of struggle, I didn't know what was.

"Was there a note?" I asked.

"No," she acknowledged. I waited.

"I'm trying to find out what happened," she said. "Do you understand that?"

"Have you spoken to Roger?" I asked.

"Who?" She had to know. Probably she couldn't say. Something about leading the witness. If that's what I was. I felt the choker around my neck again—evidence—and wondered if that's why Gina had sent it to me. A voyeur, Gina had named me, but was there really such a difference between that and a witness? *We can't all be exhibitionists*, I'd told her once. *Someone has to stay in the shadows to watch.* Maybe she'd believed me. Trusted me with it.

"Roger at Xandu's," I repeated. "He's dealing in kids, you know." I'd told her that already. "He's more than your run-of-the-mill nasty guy."

Detective Warren nodded and wrote that down. "Nasty guy," I imagined in her notes. "More than run-of-the-mill." As she wrote, I could see Gem. Just her face. Her unblinking eyes. And her brains on the walls, floor and ceiling.

I was sick then. Humiliatingly, wretchedly sick. Detective Warren pretended it was OK, natural even, that she'd seen worse plenty of times, but I couldn't look at her as she brought me wet towels.

"Ready?" George asked.

I was alone in the room where Detective Warren had deposited me. There was a chair, a table and a window, only the window didn't open. Detective Warren had given me a glass of water, a cup of coffee, and told me to try to rest.

I drank the water, closed my eyes and saw Gem, her brains flying out of her shattered skull. I opened my eyes and sipped at the coffee. It was thin, acid, covered with a layer of grease. I forced myself to swallow and saw Roger, his greasy eyes first, then his greasy neck. The white pulsing vein I would slice and the oil that would pour from it. I closed my eyes and it was all Roger, pouring out oil. So much oil that the floor was covered in it and I couldn't get away without slipping, sliding, losing my footing and falling, down, down, until I was swimming for my life in thick slimy oil.

"Ready?" George asked, and I opened my eyes.

I would have to take George, I thought. Tonight, preferably. Just to get past Pig Eyes, just to get through the front door without being thrown into the street. I would wear a wig. And a dress—I still had one, forest green, from the days when I thought that brought out the colour of my eyes. I'd hold on to George's arm, and look down as we passed Pig Eyes. He was probably used to that, women who looked down. And then, safely inside, I'd ask to see Roger.

"I want to go to Xandu's tonight," I told George.

We were outside, at the corner of Main and Hastings. A light drizzle was falling and a skinny girl was pushing an empty shopping cart down the middle of the street while a line of cars honked behind her.

"What for?" George asked.

"I need to see Roger."

"Don't be an idiot."

I would say I needed to talk to him. In private. He'd be curious, slime me with his eyes, a thick smile spreading his lips, and invite me back to his office. Maybe snap his fingers for a rum-and-Coke to take with us. I wouldn't waste any time. I had no questions. I'd look around, my hands reaching into my purse for the knife while his eyes followed mine. Handle in my palm—wood, maybe plastic—I'd pull it out and plunge. It wouldn't be hard. Skin is thin. He wouldn't struggle. Just his eyes. I'd stay to watch his eyes. Frightened, then pleading, then still as the marbles in Gina's boxes, shattered beneath their undisturbed surface. I'd take them, edge them out with a melon scoop. I'd be careful not to slip on the oil on my way out.

George unlocked the passenger side for me, opened the door, then walked around to his side. I had a melon scoop, but no wig, I realized. No purse either. I wondered where I might find them before evening. Gina would have them, but who else? I tried to think. And a knife. I had to find the right knife. I had no idea what was right. A carving knife like George used on beef? A chopping knife? A hand scythe, maybe. Like the angel of death, only smaller.

"What kind of knife killed that man in the dumpster?" I asked George.

"What do you mean?"

There were tendons, I realized. Probably thick ones. I wondered if they were behind or in front of the vein I had to cut.

"What kind of knife would slit a person's throat?"

George did a strange thing then. He took my hand in his and covered it with his other hand. They were big hands, warm and rough. I felt that if I were smaller, I could curl up in them and sleep.

He kept my hand, and as long as he had it, all I could think of was sleep. I knew I should draw away, but I couldn't. This is what hypothermia feels like, I told myself. You're cold for so long, then in one instant, you're over the line. Misery is replaced by drowsiness, a drowsiness so warm and welcoming that you can't possibly resist. *Resist*, I told myself. There was tomorrow for sleep. There was the rest of my life. But still, I couldn't draw my hand away.

George dropped it to start up the car.

"What did she tell you?" he asked.

Who, I wondered, then remembered. Detective Warren, the last hope, I had thought. The only.

"She said they hadn't ruled out foul play."

"Useful of them," George said. He placed his two hands on the steering wheel and stared straight ahead. "What did she say about Gina?"

"Not much."

She'd asked questions about Gina mostly, expressed her concern again, told me at one point that they couldn't rule out foul play with Gina's disappearance either.

Of course it was foul play, I'd wanted to shout at her. Even if Gina had made it to safety, there was still foul play. A trail of foul play that would probably lead back to her earliest childhood, if anyone cared to follow, though I suspected no one would.

"Gem was shot once. Through the mouth," I said to George.

"Warren told you that?" he asked.

I nodded.

"Why?"

"I guess she wanted to let me know Gina was in real danger. Like I might not have figured that out yet. So I would talk to her."

"Did you tell her anything?"

"I told her to go talk to Roger."

George nodded. The car was running, but George couldn't seem to decide where to drive. We idled in our parking space.

"Apparently, they thought Gem was a suicide at first," I said.

"Apparently?"

"I guess it was set up that way."

"What clued them in?"

"I don't know. She didn't tell me."

George nodded again. "We may never see Gina again, you know."

I knew that.

"And if something did happen to her, we'll probably never find out."

"What do you mean?"

"I mean, no one's going to take the trouble to set up a suicide for someone like Gina. With Gem—well, Gem was different. She was a lawyer, for one thing. A fucking former Crown Attorney. But Gina . . . Do you have any idea how many women in her line of work have gone missing from this city in the last few years?"

"Ten?" I said.

"Try thirty. At least. That we know about."

I wondered how George knew about it.

"No one would need to stage a suicide to erase someone like Gina."

There was nothing I could say to that. A simple statement. The truth, I supposed. I looked at George. I could see him swallow. My own mouth was dry and sour. I wished we had some water in the car. Some tea. Sweet, milky tea. I felt ashamed for wanting it at a time like this. Commonplace. Alive.

"Do you want some tea?" I asked. He nodded.

"The Ovaltine?"

He nodded again and started to drive.

17

"*Gina liked it* here," I told George as the first swallow of tea hit my veins. "She said it gave her a sense of history." I wondered if that was the truth, or if it was just another tidbit she'd picked up and tried on—like any of her costumes—to see how it fit. I half dreaded George's answer, his *Actually, I'm the one who likes the Ovaltine.*

He nodded. "She thought she'd been born in the wrong time. She was always saying that: 'I missed my time in history, George.' "

Who hadn't, I wondered. Who had the cosmic aim or luck to hurtle down from wherever and hit their time and civilization spot-on?

"She wanted to be a nun," I said.

He smiled and shook his head. "She never told me that."

"Actually, a saint is probably more what she meant. She said she thought she could get used to having a marble statue of herself in some town and people making pilgrimages to kiss her feet."

"Oh yeah? Whereabouts? Prince George, maybe? Kamloops?"

We both smiled, thinking of Gina as the patron saint of Kamloops.

"I think somewhere in Italy or the south of France is more what she had in mind," I said.

He shook his head again. "She told me she would have done better when the world was flat."

I nodded, could see it, the appeal of being able to walk right up to the edge of things, peer over, leap . . . a perfectly executed dive —eternal this time—into the thrill of the fall.

"Want something to eat?" George asked.

I shook my head. He couldn't help making a few suggestions. All breakfast items, though it was early evening. I wondered if George had forgotten that we had already had our few hours of light, that we were ending a day, not beginning one.

"Their oatmeal's pretty decent," he said. "None of that instant crap."

"Why did you come looking for her with me?"

He tilted his head to the right, then to the left, then rotated it slowly all the way around, as if trying to untie a large tight knot. "I don't know," he said. "I think I just couldn't stand waiting here anymore."

"So you didn't really think we'd find her. You knew she hadn't gone after Gem."

He shrugged. "She could have. She'd been looking for her."

"For the photo."

He nodded. "So she said. I guess it's the only picture she had of herself as a kid. She must have given it to Gem during the trial or something—I'm not sure—but she wanted it back." He smiled. "I wouldn't have minded seeing it myself. I bet she was one cute kid."

We were both quiet for a few minutes, drinking our tea, trying to imagine Gina as a kid.

"It's strange how much she wanted that picture back," George said after a while. "I'm not saying that's really why she was look-ing for Gem, or that that's the only reason, but really, Tova, it was like she was obsessed with that photo. I didn't get it."

I thought about it as the waitress brought us more hot water.

"Maybe that's all she had," I said. "Of her childhood, I mean."

"Maybe."

I thought about the contents of the cartons she'd left for me, and what could have been from her childhood. *Black Beauty. Jane Eyre.* Some fried marbles.

"How old was she when it was taken?"

"I don't know. A kid."

"But how old a kid? Twelve? Two?"

"I don't know, Tova. What difference does it make?"

I remembered watching my father snip the photos of my mother. He was neat about it. One cut down the centre of her face. Another across. I watched, telling myself that I would get them out of the trash later, later that night, when he was asleep, I would sneak down to the kitchen, pull them out of the trash and put them all together again. Each image he destroyed I put back together in my mind. Until he lit the match.

"It makes a difference if that's all she had left. I can understand why she might have been obsessed with it."

"It was a picture, Tova. That's all. Not her childhood. Not a letter from her parents begging her forgiveness and telling her they loved her after all. It was one stupid little picture."

"But if that's all she had . . ."

"I don't know," George said, but he didn't argue any more. "Anyway, once the man in the dumpster turned up, I don't really think finding Gina's picture could have been high on either of their lists."

I nodded my agreement.

"I'm thinking now that Roger may have been behind that first murder," George said. "Of course, if even a quarter of what Lois said was true, if it's judges and lawyers that Roger's supplying with kids, then there's no way anyone is ever going to know who was behind what. Or why. And that goes for your little detective friend, too."

"She's not my little detective friend," I said.

"Whatever. If there's some kind of private club formed with that kind of membership . . ."

"Why would Roger be behind the first murder?" I asked. "Why would he kill one of his customers?"

"Well, suppose this particular customer *was* connected to Terry —and, for all we know, other girls who've gone missing. Roger's not going to tolerate anyone who brings the cops swarming around his place. He can't afford to."

"Maybe not," I said. "But murdering a customer like that—a hot-shot criminal lawyer—I'm sure brought a lot more unwelcome attention from the cops than Terry going missing."

George raised his eyebrows. "If those shows are really private, who would even know he'd been a customer?"

"Who would tell the police, you mean."

"Right. And don't forget how that first murder was set up," he said.

I hadn't forgotten. "Like a revenge killing," I said. Personal, I had thought. Believed.

"To point the finger to someone with a particular axe to grind. By the time I picked up the rumour . . ."

"Who started the rumour that it was Gem?" I asked.

"Let's guess."

"Roger."

George nodded. "And then Gem's murder was set up to look like she'd been on the run and then killed herself . . ."

We waited for the waitress to come by with a little more hot water. She brought the bill instead.

"Doesn't it bother you?" I asked.

"Doesn't what bother me?"

"That this kind of stuff might be going on and there's the possibility they might be able to get away with it?"

He shrugged. "Sure it bothers me, but lots of things bother me." He looked at the bill. "The way I see it, there's always a few rotten boards. Always have been. Always will be. So long as the whole thing doesn't rot through." He picked up the bill again, put it down. I wondered if he'd forgotten he'd told me that theory already.

"Doesn't it bother you that it always seems to be the same rotten boards, and no one seems able to fix them?"

George shrugged and looked at the bill again. Studied it. He studied it for a long time, considering there were only two items on it.

"You want to know something?" he asked, finally, looking up. His face had gone grey. "You want to know what bothers me? I mean really bothers me? Gina being gone. That bothers me. Whatever's going on with the lawyers and the judges, I don't really care. I figure some of that's always gone on, always will. So long as it doesn't spread too wide or too deep. But Gina being gone. That bothers me. That bothers me so much that I swear to God I don't know what I'm going to do with it."

I nodded when he said it, not sure what either of us was going to do. Bake pies, most probably, I thought as I walked over to the laundromat after we parted. Wash clothes. Brew coffee. Chop onions. Chat with our customers. Or fall right through the rotten boards.

"Am I glad to see you!" Marlene said, but she didn't seem to be. Hands on her hips, face pinched and resentful, she looked like I'd abandoned her to go on a camping holiday or something, then brought home a trunkload of dead fish for her to gut and clean. I went over and hugged her anyway. She hugged me back, and when we pulled away the injured-wife-look had disappeared.

She scanned my face with a questioning look. "What happened?" she asked.

"Absolutely nothing."

"I'm sorry," she said. I didn't want her to move away, and she didn't.

"I'm so sorry," she said, again and again. It was all I needed to hear to start crying.

I told her about the trip, the uselessness of it. "It wasn't useless," she said. Rote, I knew, coming from Marlene, and wrong, no matter how much I might wish it wasn't.

It was then that I smelled it. The burning. Different from what I'd smelled in the car. Stronger. Smokier. I sniffed the air. I was sure it was real this time. I sniffed again to make sure. Marlene sniffed too.

"We've had a problem," she said. "Nothing serious. It's all taken care of now."

I looked around me and realized the place was different. All the washers were still there, the dryers, but no customers, which was odd for early evening, but not unheard of. I glanced around. The place was clean. Too clean. As if all Marlene had done since I left was scrub. And paint, I realized. That was it. She'd slapped on a coat of paint. White paint. Gleam over pallor. Maybe that's what I was smelling. Fresh paint. But there was something else too, something else seeping into me through my pores and nostrils. Smoke. I was sure of it. Beneath all the fresh paint, the gleaming walls, the sparkling chrome of the washers and dryers, there was smoke.

"What happened?" I asked.

"There was a fire," she said. "Someone set a fire," she corrected herself immediately.

"A fire?" Maybe that's what I'd been smelling all day, from way up in the Fraser Canyon. My laundromat was burning, hundreds of kilometres away, and I had smelled it. Things like that did happen from time to time, I was sure of it.

"Was anybody hurt?" I asked.

Marlene shook her head. "It was small. Just on the front porch. The only damage was smoke."

"What happened?" I asked again.

"I don't know, really. I got to work this morning and there was a fire burning on the front step."

"What do you mean? Like a bonfire?"

"Well, sort of. A large bonfire. Someone had already called the fire department. They were here within minutes so there really wasn't any damage. Not even that much smoke damage," she added, colouring a bit. "I mean, there was some damage, not just the smell, otherwise I wouldn't have closed the place and repainted. It was really grimy."

It was really grimy before the fire, I thought.

"It needed repainting," I said. Though I wouldn't have chosen white. And would have thought she could have waited for me to be here. At least check with me first. "It looks clean."

She looked around. "It's just a first coat. I thought we could go over colours together. For the second coat," she added, then said, "Oh God, I'm sorry. I'm sure it's the last thing . . . I'm so stupid. We can talk about it another time. I just . . ."

"What did the fire department have to say?" I asked.

"Nothing much. It's obviously arson. They sent a detective around. He said it didn't look like the firesetter really planned to burn the place down—he'll want to talk to you too. You know, ask

232

if there have been any odd types hanging around, what you know about the owners—all that. I'm sure they'll give Steve and Diane a hard time."

"They couldn't really think this was Steve and Diane's work."

"They always try to pin these things on the owners."

"What kind of fire was it?" I asked, though I already knew. Bits of paper, news clippings, twine. Lots of twine.

"What do you mean, what kind?"

"What was burning?"

"How would I know?" she looked at me strangely. "I didn't exactly rush in to analyze it." Then, as if she suddenly realized she might have done something wrong, might not have done her job properly: "It was really smoky. You should have seen it. Thick black smoke. I was afraid I might get smoke inhalation."

Damp paper, I thought. Damp twine. Maybe Josie did spend the odd night outside. Or maybe she'd been waiting for me out in the drizzle for a very long time.

"It sounds to me like someone was just trying to keep himself warm overnight," I said. "Or herself," I allowed. "And things got a bit out of hand."

"A bit? You should have seen it," she repeated. "The firemen were sure it was arson. And they said we were lucky. Because of the wind. It was shifting just as they got here. An hour earlier and the whole place might have gone. We were incredibly lucky."

"Do they have any suspects?" I asked, afraid of the answer, afraid, even, to imagine Josie in police custody.

"Steve and Diane, I would guess from the questions, though I doubt they're serious suspects. It was a pretty poor excuse for an arson attempt."

If that's what it was. Maybe it was a message: *Don't ever leave without saying goodbye,* maybe an attempt to keep warm. It could have been a cooking fire, even, to make coffee, since, obviously, no one else was going to.

I shouldn't have left, I thought. If Josie's locked up over this . . . I wanted to ask about Josie. What had she done the first day I hadn't shown up? We knew what she did the second. I did, anyway. Had she been in the crowd that gathered to watch? I could imagine her, kerchief pulled low, hands grimier than usual, sooty. Or maybe she wasn't the staying type, knew enough to move on when it was time. I didn't dare ask, dared only to hope that, in this case at least, I might be smarter than the cops.

"So?" George greeted me when I got to his place later that night. He looked like hell, and you wouldn't have to know him well to recognize it.

I took a stool, held out my cup for coffee.

"I'm out of pie," he told me.

"It's OK."

"There's still some cake left."

"I'll stick with a bowl of oatmeal and coffee," I said and told him about the fire. A pain in the butt, he said, but hadn't the place needed a new coat of paint? I didn't mention Josie.

"Lois come by there?" he asked, and said I must have just missed her. "She was here just a few minutes ago on her way over to the bus station. She wants to let you know she's going back up to Kamloops after all."

"Big of her to let me know," I said, disappointed.

"Nothing wrong with Kamloops," George said.

"Kamloops isn't the issue," I said, remembering Gem's tight mouth and flat eyes when she said the same thing to me.

"Maybe she'll be better off there," George went on. "It's smaller . . ."

I raised my eyebrows, felt my nostrils flaring.

"She really couldn't stick around here, you know."

"I know," I said, Roger pulsing again in my mind.

George shrugged. "She may end up OK."

"If she's lucky," I said, OK suddenly revealing itself as a promised land only the lucky could get to.

George moved the bowl of creamers next to me. "Also, another friend of yours just called here. Dara," he said with the slightest questioning raise of his eyebrows.

"Yeah. I gave her your number," I said.

"Do I look like your private secretary?"

"Sorry."

"So who is she?"

"Maybe you'll meet her soon."

He reached for menus and the coffee pot and went to do his rounds. When he came back with my oatmeal I told him about Gina's feathers. The missing ones. The hawk feather and the white tuft from the snowy owl. He opened the top two buttons of his shirt, enough for me to see them hanging low on his chest from the chain he always wore, then buttoned himself up again.

"Probably Lois has *Women Who Run with the Wolves*," I said. "Star." I poured milk and honey on my oatmeal and ate it slowly, savouring its sweet blandness.

"George," I said. There must have been something in my voice that made him stop what he was doing and meet my eye. "Do you know who the judge was at that trial?"

"Oh no," he said.

"No, what? You don't even know what I'm thinking."

"Yes I do, and I think you should just let this drop now. The cops are involved. You've told them about Roger."

"Gina sent me those clippings for a reason, George."

"Not so you could get yourself killed over it."

"Oh please. I'm not like her. I don't go about things the way she does. And she knew that." She trusted me with that.

George shook his head.

"I'm not going to do anything stupid," I said. "I just want to know—I mean, the guy who was charged is dead, the lawyer for the defense is dead, the Crown Attorney is dead. One of the witnesses is missing—I don't know about the other five." Dara could help me look into that, I thought, scanning old newspapers for any kind of identifying information about the other teenagers. If I called her now, she might have the information for me tomorrow. "I just want to find out who that judge was."

George was still shaking his head as I went to make my call.

Vicki Trerise

NANCY RICHLER was born in Montreal and now makes her home in Vancouver, B.C. Along the way she has lived in Boston, Boulder and Toronto. Her short fiction has appeared in *Room of One's Own*, *Fireweed*, *ACM* (*Another Chicago Magazine*), *The New Quarterly* and *The Fiddlehead*. *Throwaway Angels* is her first novel.

Press Gang Publishers has been producing vital and provocative books by women since 1975.

A free catalogue of our books in print is available from Press Gang Publishers, #101 - 225 East 17th Avenue, Vancouver, B.C. V5V 1A6 Canada

80025 75540